T0090444

Growing Up

Life on a Wisconsin Farm

Tom Fortney

Order this book online at www.trafford.com
or email orders@trafford.com

Most Trafford titles are also available at major online book retailers.

Printed in Victoria, BC, Canada.

ISBN: 978-1-4269-2914-4

Our mission is to efficiently provide the world's finest, most comprehensive book publishing service, enabling every author to experience success. To find out how to publish your book, your way, and have it available worldwide, visit us online at www.trafford.com

Trafford rev. 5/13/2010

 www.trafford.com

North America & international
toll-free: 1 888 232 4444 (USA & Canada)
phone: 250 383 6864 ♦ fax: 812 355 4082

For my siblings, Fredric, David and Sue,
with all the memories, joys and heartaches
of growing up together

Contents

Photographs

Acknowledgments

I want to thank my cousin Charlane Tygum for the many hours she put in proofreading, editing, typing and perfecting the manuscript for this book. My appreciation also goes out to my cousin Carolyn Solverson for working on the pictures. She took old snapshots, lightened and darkened them where necessary, and resized them to the same or better sizes. Some of these snapshots were more than seventy years old and probably were taken with a Brownie box camera. Last but not least my heart goes out to my family, especially my wife, Jane, for being so patient when I read first drafts aloud to them over and over.

Tom Fortney

Preface

<u>Growing Up</u> is about the formative years of four children who grew up on a dairy and tobacco farm in southwest Wisconsin in the 1930s and 1940s. We took our first innocent childhood steps in the security of a loving family. As we grew toward adolescence, the world was no longer a storybook land, as we had imagined in grade school, but a whole new world of different people and strange surroundings. It always seemed, though, as we went from puberty to young adulthood, that what we had learned in Sunday School and from our parents came to the surface when we were faced with making hard decisions in an adult world. The difference between right and wrong, instilled in us from earliest childhood, stayed with us all our lives.

All parents want their children to have a better life than their own, and our parents did everything they could to convince us to get a more complete education. I did not go to college like my sister and brothers, but attended a vocational school in La Crosse, Wisconsin, where I learned auto mechanics and welding. After one year, I was drafted into the Army and served in Korea. The war had just ended, so I did not see battle. I was a wheel vehicle mechanic. Serving in the United States Army was a very good experience for me, as I worked with all kinds of people, including well educated men and some who were borderline illiterate. I won't go into detail here as my Army years are an inspiration for another story for another day.

Come join us on a trip down Memory Lane.

Tom Fortney

Caution!

Duplicating some of these adventures
could be hazardous to your health

Growing Up On The Farm

When my brothers and sister and I were growing up on the farm back in the 1930s and 1940s, we found so many fun things to do that we would not have had time for TV and Game Boy and such. My brother Fred was a year-and-a-half younger than me. My sister, Sue, was four years younger and David was seven years younger. Sue and David were playmates and Fred and I were playmates.

We played "farm" on the roadside. Outside our lawn fence was a bank about one hundred feet long that we dug up with our farm toys and implements that we made from old hoes with broken handles, scrapers, and other imaginary attachments for our toy tractors. I had a farm and Fred had a farm, complete with barns and silos. We had imaginary cows and horses. We planted crops, too. The problem with corn was that it grew way too tall to be the same scale as our toys.

Fred, David, Sue and Tommy playing "on the roads"

1

Our next expansion was to build ponds and dig wells. My pond was in the road ditch and it was built from corncobs and mud. I carried the water from the milk house. It really was a muddy mess! My well was an old pail that we dug down in the ground. All ponds have frogs, turtles and fish in them. For some reason these little creatures either escaped from my pond or died.

When our cousins David and Beverly Woolhiser from Stoddard, Wisconsin, came to stay, we really played hard. We made "plans" the night before and got up before daylight, sneaking out of the house before anyone else awakened, and playing hard all day. To paraphrase Jeff Foxworthy from a 2008 morning TV show about his book <u>Dirt on My Shirt</u>, "If Mother stopped you at the door and commanded you to undress outside and take a shower before you could have supper, you knew you'd had a good day."

When you play on the farm and the folks tell you don't do that or don't go there, their most likely reason is that they don't want you to get hurt, but that is an invitation to go and explore and see what it is that they really don't want you to see.

Sometimes you had to learn the hard way. The phrase, "stepped on a nail," brought mixed feelings to little boys because they all remembered themselves or others having done that. One summer when cousin David Woolhiser was visiting, my mother noticed that he was limping a bit and asked him what was wrong. He replied, "Oh, nothing," but she was suspicious. Later she noticed his limp had become much worse and that he was growing pale and listless. She demanded that he "come into the house right now," so she could check him out. Grudgingly he limped inside and she took his temperature. It was 103.6 degrees. Now she was really concerned. When she touched his left leg he flinched. She said, "Take off your boot. I want to see your foot." He reluctantly agreed, but his foot and leg were so swollen that she could hardly pull the boot off. The boot was full of blood and David's foot was turning purple. A bad puncture wound was the cause.

She said sternly, "I want to know exactly what happened. Tell me the truth!"

Finally David confessed. We had been playing in the tobacco shed that morning and he had stepped on a board with a nail sticking up. It had gone clear through his foot, leaving a nasty wound. Infection quickly set in and spread to his leg. David admitted that he hadn't wanted to tell anybody because that would have cut into our play time.

My mother was a registered nurse before marriage and now she went into action. She bathed David's wounded foot and loosely wrapped it, saying, "We are going up to Dr. Lauder's right now and take care of your foot." We had a hired girl at that time and she watched the rest of us kids while Mother took cousin David to the doctor.

When they got home again, David went to bed and slept the rest of the day. Dr. Lauder had given him a tetanus shot and sulfa medication for the infection. Mother gave the rest of us kids a stern lecture about being more careful and reporting any injury immediately.

My brother Fred seemed to be the one who got hurt most often. One summer Reverend Frederick Dahl's youngest children stayed with us for several days. We were playing outside and Gilroy Dahl found an empty glass bottle. He said, "Back home in Baldwin when we find an empty bottle we always break it." He threw the bottle at the big maple tree in our yard and the bottom half broke off. Fred happened to be running past the tree just at the wrong time. The rest of the bottle fell on top of his head and stuck right in. He sat down on the ground and screamed and screamed. Blood gushed from his head and ran down in his eyes and all over his clothes. He was a sorry sight to behold!

By this time Mother and Gilroy's sister, Sylvia, came running. Fred needed a doctor, but the problem was how to get him there. My dad was someplace with the pickup truck and the hired man was on the back side of the farm cultivating corn. Our car, a 1929 Plymouth, was not very roadworthy.

Sylvia said, "Why don't we take the hired man's car? I think I can drive it." My mother, who was performing first aid on Fred, told Sylvia, "Absolutely not!" Sylvia was barely fourteen years old, did not have a driver's license and the hired man's car was a Model A Ford coupe, a challenging car to drive. Mother did not like the old Plymouth because it was not dependable, but she drove it anyway and took Fred to Dr. Lauder's office to get his head sewn up. Sylvia stayed home and did her best to keep us boys out of trouble.

Cousin Gilroy came down and stayed in the area later in his teens. He was wild as a boy, but wilder still in high school. In fact, he felt he was God's gift to little women, and girls were all he thought about. Somehow he had a date with a different girl almost every night. Fred and I were not old enough to date yet. Actually, Gilroy wasn't either, but that made no difference to him. He almost talked my cousin Elizabeth into eloping with him. She came to her senses and stopped the plans before she got into something that could have turned into a disaster. Gilroy's father was a Lutheran minister at Baldwin, Wisconsin, and I am sure Gilroy was one reason Reverend Dahl's hair turned gray. Gilroy never married. He worked at different jobs in California and died before he was forty-five years old. He was poorly and spent the last two years of his life with his mother, Nettie Dahl.

Kittens

When we were little, we all loved to play with kittens. For some reason all the mother cats seemed to have kittens every spring. We didn't know why, they just did. Kittens appeared throughout the year, of course. You never knew when a new batch of kittens was about to be born until they just appeared.

In the barn under the horses' mangers, chaff from the hay fell down through the cracks in the bottom. Behind these piles of chaff was a dark space almost like a cave. Mother Cat would crawl in there and give birth. We couldn't crawl back in there ourselves, so we had to wait until the kittens grew big enough to crawl out on their own. By that time they were so wild that you couldn't catch them. If you cornered a kitten and grabbed it, you would get two hands full of claws and teeth. Those little suckers could really bite. They could bite clear through our little fingers. Man, did that hurt! We didn't tell Mother about getting bitten, though. She would have scolded us and the hired men would have called us sissies. That wouldn't do. We just washed off the blood and kept quiet.

Another cat had kittens, but they were born in the hay mow, where we found them the next day. We picked them up and petted them and played with them. The next night we went back to play with them again, but the nest was empty. Mother Cat had moved them someplace else where they would be safe from little boys. We never saw them again. I don't know what happened to them.

Sometimes a stray tomcat will hunt out kittens' nests and kill all the babies, even if the kittens are his own. We could not understand why he would do this. When we got older our dad told us, "If the tomcat kills the kittens, the mother cat will come into heat, and he can breed her again." This seemed so cruel, but you can't explain why nature does some things.

My sister, Sue, was a cat lover. As the only girl she was able to get her way about different things. Some of her cats got to live in the basement. Others got to come upstairs. Dad said, "She is my only daughter and I have the right to spoil her any way I want." If we boys had brought cats in the house, they would have been thrown out.

On Saturday morning we all had "duties" around the house. Fred dusted around the rooms and I ran the vacuum cleaner. Sue didn't have to do anything since she was the spoiled girl. David was too little to help. It seemed that Fred and I had to do all of Saturday's cleaning.

One Saturday morning when I was vacuuming the living room and Susie was playing in there with her cats, I got to thinking about what might happen if I stuck a cat's tail in the vacuum cleaner. Maybe the cat would like it. I wasn't ready for what happened. When I sucked up its tail, the cat screamed like I had never heard before, climbed up Susie's back and ended on top of her head with all claws dug in and screaming at the top of its lungs. Susie started to scream, too, and this scared the other cats. Two of them climbed up the drapes clear to the ceiling and both began screaming. This started a horrible chain reaction. Mother and Aunt Mary came running to see what was happening. Fred ran upstairs and hid and I was lucky to escape with my hide still intact.

Once I got outside I stayed there until suppertime. By that time everyone had cooled down. No one ever mentioned this adventure again, but Mother was very cool around us boys for a time. I sometimes wondered if maybe I was related a little bit to Tom Sawyer.

Puppies

The first dog I can remember was a female hound that our hired man brought to the farm one day. We named her Spot because that was the name of Dick and Jane's dog in our first reader at school. Mother did not approve of a female dog. She said, "Just wait, there will be trouble." We kids did not understand what she meant.

It seemed Spot had a lot of friends, because that winter all the dogs in the neighborhood came over to visit her. They actually wore a path across our lawn right past the new blue spruce tree that Dad had planted the year before. Those dogs always stopped at the spruce and marked their territory. For some reason by spring this poor tree was dead. Also by spring the dogs stopped visiting, as Spot was no longer interested in them. She had new interests—nine to be exact. We played with her pups every night. She gave birth to them under the horse manger in the barn where the mother cat had had her kittens. Spot dug a hole out through the chaff and we could see the pups right away.

Our dog Spot with Beverly Woolhiser, Tom
and Fred Fortney, David Woolhiser

These lovable pups grew fast. We fed them table scraps from the house and skim milk from the separator. When they got big enough, Spot took them outside with her to explore the world. Mother took some pictures of us and the pups.

One night when we came home from school we could only find one male pup. We looked everywhere to no avail. Dad told us that Spot and the rest of the pups had run away and he didn't know where they were. Fathers are always right so we did not question what Dad said. Most of that summer, though, when we went anyplace in the car, we looked longingly for Spot and her puppies. Many years later we finally realized that the dog family had been "eliminated" while we were at school that day.

Spot's babies with Fred, Sue and Tom

The one remaining pup needed a name, though, and we decided to call him Doggy. It was not a spectacular name, but we loved him anyway. Doggy went wherever we boys went, whether out to the fields or to the woods. He was our constant companion. One night when there was a full moon and we were playing in our room, we heard a strange sound outside. It seemed to be coming from Mother's lower flower garden. We asked Aunt Mary, who was living with us at that time, and she said, "That sounds like a wolf!"

We were fit to be tied. We listened again and decided that maybe if we looked out another window carefully we could see what a wolf looked like. The moonlight was so bright, you could see almost everything. We got real brave and pulled back the curtains and looked out and what we thought was a wolf was Doggy. It must have been the first time he had bayed at the moon and he even surprised himself with his newfound voice.

Dogs

Doggy may have been just a dumb hound, but to us he was our own friend who unquestioningly accepted us no matter what. Doggy was about four years old. He was our constant companion wherever we went and whatever we did.

One summer we were playing over by the woods and there stood a tall oak tree along the edge of the field that needed climbing. By the time I got to the top I was probably forty-five feet off the ground and had a bird's-eye view of the world. The hired man was mowing hay with the team of horses and I saw Doggy walking around and thought to myself, he is smart enough to watch out for himself. Wrong! As the mower approached, Doggy got out of the way by walking into the uncut hay. I quickly saw that a disaster was about to happen and that I was helpless to do anything to change the outcome. Doggy was right in the path of the mower. The hired man saw him, but too late. You can't stop a team of horses on a dime. Too late. Doggy lost a leg in the hay mower and I had seen it all happen.

Later Mother said, "You have to kill him, put him out of his misery." We wouldn't hear of this and Dad, being soft-hearted and compassionate, said, "With our care, he will heal up and be able to walk on three legs."

Sure enough he did and we had him for another year. Doggy succumbed to another condition that kills a lot of farm dogs. It is called "got run over by the milk truck." This scenario is almost always fatal. We now had lost our friend who had been around for about half of our lives.

Dad said, "We will get another dog for the children." The new dog was a puppy about two months old. He was a long-haired black and white dog of unknown parentage, but that did not matter. He was ours and that was the most important. We named him Tippy.

My sister, Sue, and baby brother, David, were inseparable friends and they always played together. They were exploring all of the farm just as Fred and I had done. One day they were playing down by the road. In those days the patrolmen didn't mow along the road or cut brush like they do nowadays and in most places there was just enough room to meet another car. Cattle trucks seemed to trim the leaves off overhanging trees and in some places you were going through a green tunnel. These tunnels were exciting adventure spots for kids. All of a sudden the milk truck went by terribly fast. We heard brakes squealing, saw the truck go sideways and heard milk cans crashing. Then everything was silent except for the sound of Sue crying her heart out.

Our first terrifying thought was that David had been hit and was lying dying or dead down there on the road. Mother ran down the road to the accident scene, but Dad took a shortcut across the hog pasture. He must have been running on straight adrenaline because he cleared both fences like a deer and got there in no time flat. David was okay but scared. Sue was heartbroken because Tippy lay dead on the road and she had seen it all happen. Tippy had stepped out of the weeds right in front of the truck.

Mother's terror now turned to blind anger as she verbally attacked Harold, the milk truck driver, and told him he didn't have an ounce of good sense and drove way too fast for the road even when there were no children around. Harold was badly shaken and did not need this tirade. We no longer had a dog and there was once again an empty place in our lives.

Then one summer day our neighbor Alfred Henrikson came over with a dog. He told us that Kenneth Dewitt had stopped by and asked him to kill a dog that he had. The dog was what you would call a yellow cur. He was short-tempered and had one short leg, as a result of being run over by a car. Alfred told us he was taking the dog over in the field with his rifle in hand to "eliminate" him when he remembered that Freddy Fortney didn't have a dog and maybe he would take him.

We named him Cappy, short for Captain. One problem: Cappy never forgave Alfred for almost killing him. When Alfred came around, Cappy would snarl and growl at him and one time he added insult to injury by peeing on Alfred's leg and then scratching his feet in the grass, as you may have seen dogs do. Alfred said, "I should have shot that S.O.B. when I had a chance." Cappy never forgot Alfred and growled at him whenever he was near.

Susie and her cats and Cappy, the dog with an attitude

Cappy had three hate objects. Number One of course was Alfred Henrikson. Number Two was our dad's brother, Malvin Fortney. Uncle Malvin came over one morning real early. In fact, no one was up yet. Cappy had stayed in the house all night. Malvin came right in without knocking and was met by a growling and snarling Cappy. He wouldn't let him go across the kitchen or get out the door until my dad came down and defused the situation.

Cappy's Number Three enemy was Harold Dregne, the milkman. Harold purposely dropped a milk can on Cappy and promptly got bitten in the leg. Cappy definitely was a dog with an attitude.

One time Aunt Mary was babysitting at our house when the folks went to some party. Sue cried and cried because Mother was gone. She just would not shut up and wanted to get out the door and go and find Mother. Aunt Mary said, "Don't go out that door or the wolves will get you and eat you alive." Sue didn't believe her and thought Aunt Mary was just trying to scare her. Sue opened the door and there on the step was Fritz, Sully Dregne's big German police dog. Fritz looked just like a big vicious wolf! Aunt Mary didn't know Fritz was there, and it didn't help any when she said, "See? I told you so!" Sue got so frightened that she lost her voice and held her breath until she turned blue. I actually felt sorry for her, even if it was kind of funny. Sue never looked out the door on a dark night again.

Dog stories go on and on. Many years later we had a Saint Bernard named Joe. He came from DeSoto, Wisconsin. Joe was very big. He would jump on you and put his paws on your shoulder, then lick your face. The people that had him wanted to get rid of him because he was always getting loose and they were afraid he would get hit by a car and they would get sued. Here we went again, rescuing a dog from being "eliminated."

Joe was a friendly lovable dog, but he was a vagabond and went hiking to see the world all by himself, time after time. We put a cow bell on Joe. Then he disappeared for a week. When he came back the cow bell was missing. The next time he went away he came back in ten days and the cow bell was back on his collar. How the heck could that happen? Only Joe knew. Joe chased up a young rabbit one day and chased him around the shed. When he caught up to the rabbit he grabbed him and swallowed him whole, then stopped and coughed up the poor bunny again. It was still kicking but had died of fright. It was like the Biblical Jonah being swallowed by the whale.

Joe didn't live long. He jumped on Charlie Monson's dog one day when he drove through our yard with his tractor. The two dogs rolled in front of the big tractor tires. Charlie couldn't stop his tractor in time and both dogs died. This was a different version of "got run over by the milk truck." You just substitute tractor for milk truck.

They say you should always keep your dog tied up. Would you like to be chained to a stake in the ground for the rest of your life? Farm dogs are part of the family and should have the run of the place. Even if your dog is not too smart he will develop a strong instinct to guard his family and farm all the time, especially at night. We completely trusted our dogs to guard us. Most farmers leave their cars and trucks unlocked with the keys in them all the time and never lock their houses either. Whether you have a Joe, Shep, Ole Yellow or Cappy, you will always be safe.

Grandma Karn

Our grandmother, Karn Marie Fortney, was a fantastic housekeeper. Her sheets and pillowcases were whiter than white because she boiled them in "bluing" and ironed them all before putting them away. She did not trust hired girls, either, to boil the clothes or do the ironing.

Grandma Karn could not sleep in the morning so she chased the men and boys outside to do chores and then she went to work in the house. When they came back in for breakfast, there would be stacks of buckwheat pancakes, bacon and salt pork, as well as sorghum molasses and honey, coffee and buttermilk, plus fresh wild berries in season.

Karn and Ole T. loved to have company in their new house, which they built in 1917. When their son Alfred married Ruby Jasperson, the young couple went to North Dakota on their honeymoon. Karn decided that when they got back, it would be a good time to show off the new bride. She made plans to have Ladies Aid in their home when the newlyweds returned and she invited everyone. The second day after Fred and Ruby returned, Ladies Aid was held and five hundred people came. They arrived in the afternoon and stayed until late at night. Ruby was totally overwhelmed! Never in her life had she seen so many people in one place, especially in someone's home.

Often company came from North Dakota, Dunn County or Richland County, Wisconsin, and stayed for two weeks. The men pitched in with field work and the women with housework and canning. In the evening more company would come over for a lot of visiting and a superb lunch. Those of us who are old enough to remember those days kind of miss them, but we realize it would be impossible to do today, since most people have a job off the farm and are so programmed that it would not be feasible.

Another thing we remember about Grandma Karn is her love for her flowers. In a flower bed south of our house, we have a lilac bush that Karn planted in 1902. Circling the lilac are peony bushes and lily of the valley that she planted at the same time. These plants and flowers are still growing and blooming today.

Karn always carried a hoe when she was outside. It was partly to help her balance, though she would never admit it. She said, "If I have a hoe with me, I can chop off a weed if I see one, and when I go to the woods to pick berries, my hoe will come in handy to chop the head off a rattlesnake. Or to whack a wolf!"

Our fondest memories were of sitting on her lap or rocking on her knee and having her teach us to say table grace in Norwegian. She had a radio in the dining room next to her house plants and would spend hours listening to religious programs and music while rocking in her favorite rocking chair. If she did not have a child sitting on her lap, she was mending socks or patching overalls.

After Ole T. passed away, on December 27, 1935, Karn suffered from rheumatism and had a hard time getting around. Later she had a heart spell and spent several months in bed. In the spring of 1939 she tended her beloved flowers every day, but on May 9, 1939, she died of a stroke in the night. Several of the flower varieties that she nursed through the years died soon after she did. We were all small children and did not understand death and were devastated by the loss of our beloved grandmother. My sister, Sue, who was three-and-a-half years old, ran away and was found down in the cow pasture, looking for Grandma.

When Fred and Ruby got married, Ruby could not understand all the company and food preparation at the Fortneys. At the Jaspersons, after Ruby's father, Andrew, passed away, they lived very frugally. They paid cash for any food item purchased or they did without. Sophia sold eggs and cream and those were the source of all their living expenses. The Jaspersons probably spent less than $40 or $50 a year on food and groceries. The Fortneys spent $50 per month and charged it!

Sweet memories of parents and grandparents are what connect us with the past as we build for the future.

The New Car

The family car when we were young children was an old Plymouth, a 1929 model. Dad said, "It was already wore out when it was delivered new."

In reality it was a poor car. It didn't drive well, was almost impossible to start in the wintertime and seemed to have an "attitude" like it did not like people, if that were possible. Dad had a small pickup and a medium sized truck. The pickup was a rare vehicle, a four cylinder Buick with a cloth top and a very small box. About all you could haul in it was a couple of calves, or if you went to town, two or three cases of eggs. The truck was a Stoughton with high wheels and a flat platform with side racks.

Dad's new 1936 GMC pickup in a 1937 snowstorm

In the spring of 1936 Dad cured a lot of problems at once. He bought a new GMC pickup truck. He traded in both the Buick pickup and the Stoughton truck for it. This new pickup was a beautiful green color with black fenders and yellow wheels. We were so proud of it. It actually became our first choice for a family car. I would sit in the middle when we first got this beautiful new pickup and Fred would sit in Mom's lap. That same year Sue was born, in October, so Fred and I sat side by side in the middle and Mom held Sue. In 1939 David was born and things started to get a little crowded. One of us boys had to stand up in the middle. We were all growing real fast and the pickup was getting real crowded.

In about a year we got rearranged. Mom held baby David in her lap, Sue sat in the middle, Fred stood up and I had to sit on the outside between Dad and the driver's door. Dad said one night, "The pickup is getting much too crowded and I think we should get a new car so there is room for our family." Fred said, "I want a purple car."

A roadside picnic on a trip to Illinois in the 1941 Pontiac Chieftain

One night when we came home from school, there it was! A new 1941 Pontiac Chieftain! It was dark blue. Dad said, "They didn't have a purple car, but this is the next best thing." He had traded in the old Plymouth. It hadn't been started for several years and had begun to sink into the ground in the lawn by the back door where it was parked. Clark's Garage sent out a wrecker to pull it to town. There were rumors of war so scrap metal was quite valuable. If I remember right the old Plymouth brought $125 for scrap. It probably was melted down and the steel used to build a battleship that got sunk by the enemy. This would have been the end of the old Plymouth. It deserved to die.

We were all so proud of our new car. The "new car smell" was something we had never experienced before. Pickups don't smell like new cars. Dad said we needed some new clothes to go with the new car so that we looked proper. We children were so proud when we went to church. Everybody had to look over our new car. Mother said, "Don't act so proud. Remember, pride cometh before a fall." This somber saying was something that she remembered from growing up in the Jasperson family.

Dad didn't think that way. He said, "Let's celebrate and start planning some trips for the new car. We can pack coffee and milk and cookies and stop at parks along the road and have picnics."

We kids thought this would be lots of fun and we wanted to go the next day, but Mom said school came first.

The GMC pickup was now five years old. It seemed all our relations thought that now that the Fortneys had a big new car, we really didn't need a pickup anymore and they would come and borrow it for a while. One uncle borrowed it for almost all winter. The spare tire fell off uptown and he never found it back. Dad said, "Just buy a new one and forget it." Uncle grumbled and grumbled but finally bought one and then promptly returned the pickup, saying, "Keep your damn pickup then." It seemed that Dad was hauling stuff for everybody in the countryside and they all thanked him, but he never got any money for his time or for the gas. Just one of the problems of being compassionate and generous.

Climbing Trees

What red blooded young boy can resist climbing trees? By the time I was eleven years old I believe I had climbed every tree in our yard, then had gone over in the woods and climbed some of those trees, too. Some were a real challenge because the first branch was so high up in the air that we couldn't reach it. Sometimes a lower branch that grew out thirty feet or so would be closer to the ground out near its end. Cattle had reached up and eaten the leaves that they could reach. Cows can reach up about three feet higher than little boys.

Tommy at six. Big enough to climb small trees.

We thought and thought about this problem, my cousin David Woolhiser and I. We both came up with the solution at the same time. If we could find a metal rod up in the tobacco shed and bend a hook in one end, we would have a handle to hook the branch and pull it down to where one of us could grab it while the other held it down with our new tool. One problem: We found a three-eighths inch rod about four feet long, but how could we make a hook on one end? It was much too stiff to bend with our little hands. Then we spied the draw-bar on Dad's new tractor that was parked right there. If we stuck the end of the rod in the draw-pin hole, maybe we could bend it enough to make a hook. We tried and we had our hook. It worked like a charm. I pulled the branch down and David grabbed it and pulled himself up. His weight kept the branch bent down so I could pull myself up on it, too. We were ready to ascend to new heights. Getting down might be a problem, but we would think about that when the time came.

The thrill of climbing some of these large trees was just like going exploring in a wilderness. We knew about how old some of the big trees were by counting the growth rings on the stumps when Dad and the hired man cut some of them down for lumber. To make it more interesting, still growing in our woods were a few rare species of oak tree that were almost extinct. We had one in our yard, too. It was hollow and fell down in 1960. When it was cut up we cut off chunks of firewood starting at the bottom of the trunk until we came to the spot where the rot ended. At that point there were 224 rings. Assuming an oak tree takes 35 years to get to the size where the main trunk is 16 feet tall, this tree had been growing for 259 years! If you count backwards it figures that this tree grew out of an acorn in 1701. This proves that our friend the big oak was a baby 147 years before my first ancestors came to this country from Norway. How awesome! Here we were, two little boys, climbing a tree that was as old as the hills and had never been climbed by a human before. Sure, it may have been dangerous, but so what? Squirrels climbed trees and they could have fallen down, too. But we didn't let Fred climb with us because he might have gotten hurt and it would have been our fault.

The old maple tree by the windmill

After you master one big tree you naturally eyeball another tall tree to climb. Every summer we would stay at my Uncle Wallace Jasperson's for about a week. My cousins David and Beverly Woolhiser came, too. Here we found adventure after adventure. First off, some monster pine trees in the yard were just ripe for climbing. We waited until the grownups were not around so we would not get yelled at. I took one tree and David took the other. The branches were quite close together and awfully scratchy, but we were tough kids. So what if we got bloody hands or scratches on our legs. The summit of a tree mountain was so high in the air that when we looked down we saw the roofs of the house and barn so far down that we thought they looked small. We could see down into the silo, too. Uncle Wallace had one with no roof. When we looked the other way, the city of Viroqua came into plain view. Viroqua was three miles away! We were very proud of our accomplishment for the day.

The next challenge was the cedar trees around the garden. My Grandfather Andrew Jasperson had planted a row of cedars around the garden plot to protect it from storms and to make a wind break for the house. He did this when Wallace was a small child. Sadly, Grandfather Andrew died of TB when Wallace was only three years old. David and I knew that these trees had never been climbed either, so this was another challenge to master. While we climbed trees Fred and Beverly went exploring in a patch of tall horse weeds.

Up in the tree tops we discovered that if we leaned one way and then the other, we could sway back and forth about six feet. Now we imagined that we were in a jungle, playing Tarzan of the Apes. Our next challenge would be to let go at the end of the swing and jump to the next tree. If we were lucky we could go all the way around the garden tree-to-tree.

Just then in the weed patch where Fred and Beverly were playing, Fred started to scream bloody murder. Then Beverly began to scream. What was wrong? We thought someone must be hurt so we shinnied down to the ground out of our jungle trees to rescue them from whatever was the problem. It turned out that Fred had been making a path through the ten-foot tall horse weeds and crawled right into a pile of old barbed wire. One rusty end went into his leg and he thought a rattlesnake had bitten him and wouldn't let go. It was so dark in the bottom of the weed patch that you couldn't see anything, so imagination took over. All this screaming got the attention of Aunt Leone and she came running, at about the time David and I got down from the trees. Luckily there was no snake, just a terrified little boy with a bad puncture wound that didn't bleed.

Another trip to town to see a doctor was in order. A puncture wound that doesn't bleed can be very serious and Aunt Leone was not a nurse. She didn't know how to drive so she ran out in the field to get Wallace to take Fred to town. Wallace grumbled about having to go to town when he was busy. He said, "Damn spoiled brat should have known better than to get hurt." Fred got another tetanus shot and the wound was opened and a drain put in.

David and I kept quiet about climbing the cedar trees and about our Tarzan of the Jungle plans. Wallace would really have had a bird if he had known about that. My mother came up that night and took Fred home. If Wallace had known what we had been doing he would have gotten a rope and tied us to the bed post.

I Double Dare You!

As farm boys grow up, they are always testing authority to see just how far they can go. We were like all the others. Our adventures with coaster sleds and old buggy frames fit right into the picture. What was next on the agenda? How about "rock rolling"? City kids didn't have rocks and flat land people didn't have hills like we had in southwest Wisconsin.

Cousin David and I, when we stayed up at Uncle Wallace Jasperson's farm during the summers, looked over the steep hills on both sides of the valley, and at the rocks up toward the top, and we could not resist the temptation. If we got a rock loose, maybe it would roll all the way to the bottom of the hill. We started with a rock about as big as a basketball and gave it a shove from the top of the hill. It rolled all the way to the bottom and we could hear it crashing through the brush. After about ten rocks this size we started to get bored because it was just the same thing over and over. How about rolling a great big rock off the bluff?

We found one but it seemed to be part way in the ground. If we took some sharp sticks maybe we could dig away some dirt and get it loose. We dug and dug and finally we got clear under it. Now we just needed a pry bar to get it started. We found a couple of posts in a corner of Uncle Wallace's fence and we pried and pried and finally the monster rock came loose and started to roll down the hill. It gained a lot of speed and nothing would have stopped it. As it went down through the woods we heard it crashing through the brush. Then it hit a small tree, tore it out of the ground, roots and all, and rolled halfway across the valley. Afterwards we got to thinking that this could have been a disaster.

What if someone was down there and got hit by our boulder? He would have been killed. Also, Uncle Wallace's cows were in the pasture and the rock could have killed a cow. Maybe we should do something else instead.

There were some boys down at Springville, Wisconsin, who were master rock rollers and probably should have been arrested for destruction of property, but I don't think anything came of it. They were always rolling rocks and one summer day they eyeballed a big rock up on the hill above the village that was bigger than a cow. They decided to get this monster loose and let it roll. This would be the culmination of their career in rock rolling. They worked for many days getting it loose, first by digging away from the downhill side, a lot of digging because the rock was more than half buried in dirt and gravel. Next was to get it loose so it would roll. They used a couple of bumper jacks and a ten-ton hydraulic jack and then put rocks behind it so they could get a new bite with the jacks. Finally it was at a balance and ready to roll. One more push with the jacks and away it went.

The rock went horribly fast and headed straight for the highway. It bounced and went over the highway in two bounces. Then it changed course and headed in a straight line for Norma Knutson's garage. As luck would have it, Mrs. Knutson was not home. She was lucky because she always parked her new Buick in this garage. That rock went right through one wall of the garage and out the other side. It never slowed down and never stopped until it landed in the creek! If Norma's car had been in the garage it would have been totally destroyed. Except for the unplanned garage mishap this was a great rock rolling success.

Most farms had tobacco sheds and this was an intriguing place to play. You would climb up on the hanging poles and walk along the poles without hanging on. We made a game of it. The bottom hanger was only four-and-a-half feet off the ground, so we called the bottom hanger "first grade." As we got braver we climbed up to the next hanger and if you could walk a pole clear around the shed you would be in fourth grade. This continued until you got clear to the top of the shed and that was college. If you had enough guts to walk a single pole the full length of the shed and back again, you had graduated from college. We were by then twenty-four feet above the ground. We could have fallen off the pole and landed on a piece of machinery parked below, or on a pile of fence posts, and have been mortally wounded, but that was part of the game. If you didn't fall, no problem.

The hay mow of our barn was also an exciting place to play. There is a steel track the full length of the barn fastened to the very peak of the inside of the roof, and a carrier assembly with steel wheels that the carrier rides on. A heavy rope goes through an assembly of pulleys and is fastened at one end to the hay fork and out the other end to whatever is used to pull to get the hay up in the mow. When the hay fork full of hay gets up to the track, it trips a latch and a catch secures the fork in the carrier and then the load goes along the track to the end of the barn or wherever you are putting the hay. You then jerk a trip rope and the fork releases the hay. You then pull the fork back and reset it in another forkful (load). Our barn is one hundred years old and this technology was installed when the barn was built.

It is about thirty feet from the hay mow floor up to the track and a ladder is built into the end of the barn so you can climb up to service the carrier. We boys wondered what it was like inside the cupola in the center of the barn roof, right where the hay fork met the track. We wanted to find out, but Fred thought it was too dangerous to go up there. I decided to find out myself so one day in early summer, before any hay was put in, I devised a plan. I climbed up the ladder and pulled the rope so the carrier would come right up close to me. Then I stepped over on the hay fork and by pulling on the track I was able to go clear to the center of the barn and stop just before the carrier hit the trip that let the fork go down. Next was to pull myself up in the cupola. There were several pigeon nests and a lot of pigeon poop everywhere. One nest had eggs in it and two had baby birds. Next was to let myself down to the hay fork again and pull myself back to the ladder at the end of the barn. I never went up there again. Now you couldn't pay me enough to do such a dangerous thing.

When we got older, Dad let us drive the tractor to other farms where we helped at threshing time. It was almost as much fun driving over there as it was working. Our tractor, an F-20 Farmall, only went ten miles an hour. When we went down some of the hills, the temptation to push in the clutch pedal and coast was too much. We tried it and wow, would we ever go. I bet we got up to twenty-five or thirty miles per hour! This was awfully dangerous since this tractor did not have good brakes and when it was first made, the early models had steel wheels and were meant to go only four miles an hour.

Luckily we all survived these dangerous stunts and are here now to tell about them. Some of our adventures were almost like some others nowadays—hang gliding, parachuting, bungee jumping, bull riding, sky diving and racing—the unmatched thrill of impending death.

One-Wheeled Car

You probably will say, what the heck is a one-wheeled car? It is partly a child's inventiveness and partly imagination. If you take a piece of two-by-four about 3 feet long, and two boards 1 x 2 x 12 inches long, one wheel off a junk coaster wagon, a 3/8 inch x 3-1/2 inch bolt, and another board 1 x 6 x 14 inches, plus a full pail of imagination, you can build one in just a little while.

You nail the two 1 x 2 x 12 inch boards on each side of one end of the two-by-four and drill holes in the lower ends to mount the wheel with the bolt. Nail the board across the other end of the two-by-four. This is your steering wheel. If you can find some old switches to mount on your "dashboard" and draw a speedometer on the board, you are ready to start driving.

Now is where imagination comes in. You decide if you have a Cadillac, Buick, Pontiac or Ford. You make the engine sound and the shifting sound. You push your one-wheeled car over to the barn or take it along when you go down in the pasture to pick berries. A properly driven and bent nail makes a place to hang a syrup pail to bring berries home to mother as a family treat for supper. You don't need to put on chains because your one-wheeled car will never get stuck in the winter time. We had roads all over the farm yard where we could "drive" our cars. I remember going out "Dach Ridge Road."

With a healthy imagination a child never gets bored.

Hideouts and Camps

All healthy young boys seem to have a born-in instinct of the spirit of Tom Sawyer and Huck Finn. This includes exploring area rivers and lakes, and imaginary rivers, even if they are only a creek. Your young son may be partly Davy Crockett, too. When we grew up, we explored every nook and cranny of every valley that we could walk to and get home again from in a long day. Boys will also study animal tracks in the snow and other "signs."

I was thrilled beyond belief when Mom and Dad allowed me to subscribe to <u>Fur-Fish-Game</u> magazine. It was the first magazine of my own that came once a month in my own name. I read every issue from cover to cover, including all the ads. I was allowed to keep all the back issues and stored them in my bookcase.

Naturally the next thing was a fly rod and reel so that I could fish for trout. This was a vast improvement over the old willow branch pole that most boys start out with. One day recently, while looking through some old things that I had kept as treasures, to my surprise I found a record of trout I had caught over two summers, the dates, measured lengths and weights. I will always save that record and someday show it to grandchildren.

My next project after reading all the stories about hunting small game in my magazine was a .22 rifle. My dad did not hunt. He had had a bad experience when he was young and vowed never to own a gun. He had borrowed a shotgun and fired at a jackrabbit right over the head of his dog. The dog was not hit, but died of shock from the noise of the explosion. That did it for my dad. No more guns ever.

Naturally I was facing an uphill battle to convince my folks to let me own a rifle. I studied all the stories in my magazine about hunting and all the ads about rifles and had my heart set on a Marlin 81DL, an eighteen shot bolt action. I could just about feel this neat rifle in my hands and I imagined bagging squirrels and rabbits to bring home for Mom to cook for supper.

After two years my folks finally said I could have a rifle, but I would have to earn it and pay for it with my own money. I saved my allowance and helped two uncles plant tobacco. By fall I had it all saved up, $15.50, and went to "Snort" Larson's sport shop in Viroqua and he had a Marlin 81DL just like I had been dreaming about for two years.

Next the folks lectured me about how dangerous guns were and I almost felt guilty for wanting one. My cousin David had a .410 shotgun and we would plan big hunting trips to the woods in the fall when hunting season opened. We were always very careful with guns and never had a close call.

The next outdoor activity would be to do some trapping. I had about eight traps and a lot of enthusiasm. In Fur-Fish-Game they told about boiling your traps so there was no human smell in them and how to set them. You could set blind sets where the animal would just stumble into the trap and get caught or use bait of some sort or use different lures to get them to come to your sets. I bought some fox lure and it smelled terrible! I don't know why a fox or anything else would be attracted to this putrid stuff.

My trapping experience was just that, an experience. You are required to have current tags on your traps and check them every day. In the whole season I caught no foxes, one tomcat, three bluejays and one skunk. Several traps had been tripped by I don't know what. So much for trapping.

The first day of trout season was the most exciting day of the year! David and his friend Mike Roidt and I went fishing in the Bad Axe Creek near Belgium Ridge. We had been working down there in lower Wildcat Hollow, building a "cabin." We had a lot of big plans. There were thousands of rocks to use for walls and to build a fireplace, but for some reason they just did not fit together like the ones in the picture in my magazine. A lot of trees were all around, too, but after chopping for hours with our camp hatchet we were getting nowhere and had hardly got started by opening day, so decided to use the site for a camp instead.

We had brought along bacon and eggs and fruit and bread and candy bars and drinking water and coffee. If we went to the creek at daylight maybe we could catch some fish to cook for breakfast. The fish were biting hungrily and we cleaned some chubs and suckers for breakfast. We built a roaring fire, greased the frying pan with butter, and put in bacon, eggs and fish. In just a few minutes the eggs were done and we thought the bacon and fish should be done, too, so we dished it all up. The eggs were done but the rest was not, especially the fish, which were slimy and cold. Have you ever tried to eat a raw sucker? We did and it is awful. Luckily no one got sick. The candy bars tasted good so they became our sustenance for the rest of the day.

I remember a poem I read one time:

> Behold the fisherman
> Mighty are his preparations
> He riseth up early in the morning
> He returneth late at night
> Telling tall tales
> And the truth is not in him!

Ice Skating

In the winter time down at Hinkst School everybody wanted to slide, ski or skate on the ice. When we little kids saw the big kids skating on the creek, we wanted to do the same thing. We were too young to have skates, though. We thought maybe skates were not made for little boys, but in reality parents were reticent to get us skates until we were older. A wise decision. Our feet were growing so fast that shoe skates would be too small way too soon and would have to be replaced by the next year. As we grew our feet slowed down and shoe skates would fit for several years.

In the meantime we slid on the ice as best we could. If you cleaned off a strip of ice on the creek and took a good running start, then locked your legs, you could slide up to thirty feet before you stopped. You had to be careful, though. If you got too good a start you could run out of ice and go head first into the rocks along the creek. You could be wounded and would hurt for many days. But you didn't dare cry or complain. If you did, the big boys would call you a sissy and being called a sissy just couldn't happen.

Finally we were big enough for skates. One Christmas when Fred and I opened our presents we each found a pair of hockey skates. They were the answer to our prayers. We took them along to school after vacation and they were all we thought about until noon hour. We ate lunch in about two minutes, then were out the door and down to the creek. There wasn't much snow that year and the ice was smooth and clean. We imagined skating like the eighth graders did, but when we put on our skates and tried it, we couldn't stand up. We weren't going to admit defeat so we kept trying until we didn't do nose dives.

By the end of the week we could stand up quite well, but our skates had cut the ice and in places it was rough. We had heard that at the ice rink uptown they flooded the rink and a new layer of ice would freeze right down. How were we going to flood our little creek rink? We thought and thought and finally an idea sprouted. If we could raise the water level in the creek, maybe we could grow some new ice. Our little brains were working overtime to come up with ideas. Ah-ha! Maybe we could pile up some loose rocks on the downstream end of our rink and cause the water to back up over our ice. We tried and it didn't work as we planned—it worked better! New water started coming over the ice from the upper end of our rink and slowly ran over the complete area. We had new ice the next day and could skate again.

It got very cold that night, maybe fifteen degrees below zero. When we put our skates on and tried our new ice, it was so hard that our skates wouldn't cut it and they went sideways and we fell down. Was there something wrong with the new ice? When we got home that night we told Dad and he said that ice got harder and harder the colder it got, and maybe tomorrow would be another story.

The cold snap went away and the weather warmed up some so we could skate again. One problem, teacher told the little girls to go out and play. Where do you suppose they went? Right up to our skating rink and they were right in our way. Since we now felt brave with skates we tried something else. The big hill before you got to school was all covered with glare ice. The patrolman did not spread sand and it was very slippery. All the cars had to have chains in order to go anywhere.

We carried our skates up to the top of the Hinkst Hill at noon hour when teacher wasn't looking. If we could stand upright on our skates clear to the bottom and then make a lefthand turn, we could travel almost one-half mile down the valley. We put on our skates, pushed off, and took off like a shot! Fred got scared, sat down and stopped, but my buddy Carter Thompson and I flew down the hill like the wind! We were really getting scared and didn't think we could make the corner at the bottom. Fate took over. Some gravel was sticking up through the ice, caught our runners, tripped us, and we fell down, slid down the road and spun round and round. I lost my glasses and my gloves, skinned up both hands and got a bloody nose. Carter was sore and bloody, too.

Teacher had looked out the schoolhouse door and had seen it all happen. Boy, did we get a talking-to. The school had a first aid kit for emergencies like this. There was gauze and tape and something called methylate, a mixture of alcohol and iodine used to treat wounds. It made our battle scars look more important than the mercurochrome that Mother used on us at home. For some reason it seemed like teacher had to patch somebody up every few days.

When there was snow and ice, we came to school early so we could play for at least an hour before school, which started at 9:00 AM. If we hurried we could get there a little after 7:30. Teacher didn't arrive until 8:30 or later, so we could do whatever we pleased until she showed up.

Over one weekend the weather warmed up and the creek flooded. The water ran over into Harold Dregne's tobacco field. On Sunday night it got real cold again and this new little lake froze solid. What a beautiful skating rink! Across one side there was an area of glass-smooth ice almost two hundred fifty feet long. We had never seen a rink like this. Everyone was running, sliding and really having fun.

Just about then, here comes Fritz Dregne. He had walked down the hill to school. Fritz always reminded me of Huckleberry Finn, one of my childhood heroes. Fritz wore slightly ragged clothing and a long stocking cap and was whistling a Norwegian tune that he knew. He came out on the ice with both hands in his pockets. I remember Dad telling us, "Never walk on ice with your hands in your pockets because if you slip you don't have time to get them out again and catch yourself when you fall and you will get hurt."

Fritz's feet went out from under him and he fell terribly hard on his right side. His right arm now hung lopsided and he could not move it. It was broken! A very bad break. Just then teacher came. I bet she thought that her job was more like being a nurse than a teacher. She put Fritz in her car and took him home back up on the hill. We didn't see Fritz again for several days. His dad had taken him to the doctor, who set the arm and put a cast on it. Needless to say this was the end of playing on the ice for Fritz for the rest of the winter. When his arm healed up it was as good as new. We country kids were really pretty tough.

Sledding

Another winter sport that we did was sliding on the road with our sleds. I don't know why our parents allowed this. I never let my kids do it. No sand was spread on the roads, so the surface was all hard packed snow and ice. On some long hills you could go so fast that the wind brought tears to your eyes. I believe that we probably got up to fifty miles per hour. It took twenty times as long to get back up the hill as it took to get down. This was a Sunday afternoon sport. All the neighborhood boys would go sledding. We never hit a car though and thought they should all feel lucky. Six sleds might have hurt a car.

On the way home from school we would slide down the steep driveway of Sully C. Dregne's farm. His wife, Christine, grumbled about those crazy neighbor kids and when she cleaned the ashes out of the stove she spread them on the road where it went past her house. Maybe she thought she was going to spoil our sled ride. But here we came, as fast as lightning, and slid across her ashes and didn't even slow down.

We normally flew past the milk house and stopped in the deep snow in the tobacco fields below the barn. After we went past the house we spied a very serious problem. Someone had parked Sully's F-20 Farmall tractor by the milk house and completely blocked the road. We had about one-and-a-half seconds to change our course and there was only one choice. The big doors into the hay mow were open about three feet and here we came at fifty miles an hour. We turned and went right into the hay mow and landed in a big pile of loose hay. This was a whole lot better than being pasted to the draw bar in the back of that F-20 Farmall.

Needless to say Mom and Dad never found out about this and Susie was too young to come along. She probably would have tattled.

Wire fences were an irritation to us, too. Fred and I would go sledding at home after school. You could start up by the tobacco shed, go right down the driveway all the way to the mailbox across the road and then go across Uncle Malvin's hay field. Below the hay field was a three-wire fence. If you were real careful and lay flat on your sled you could go right underneath the fence, if you went under right next to the corner post. Then you went through the woods all the way to the bottom of the hill along the high bank of the big gully. By then you had slowed way down, but at one spot if you took a hard left and went down the bank into the ditch (almost straight down) you would pick up a lot of new speed and almost get to the top of the other side. A long exciting ride!

It was getting dark but I thought, why not one more sled ride. I took a good running start and practically flew down the road and across the field. It was now so dark that I couldn't see the fence. No problem, I would just follow the sled tracks and go under where we always did. Big mistake. I went under the wire, three posts to the left of the corner, where the wire was only six inches off the ground. I came to a screeching halt halfway through the fence with a barbed wire in my face and a deep gash almost all the way through into my mouth, almost to my teeth.

I thought I had cut my throat! Bleeding profusely I ran up the hill to the house and rushed inside. Aunt Mary was there and she threw her hands in the air and let out a blood curdling scream. I suppose I was a scary sight with blood all over my face, hair and clothes.

My mother the nurse reacted differently. She got out her trusty first aid kit and some wet towels and cleaned me up. She said, "We're going uptown right now and get a doctor to sew you up again." I then got a stern talking-to about being more careful and thoughtful. Mom even said, "It's a shame you disfigured yourself. You'll probably have a hard time shaving when you get old enough." I felt bad but it was too late. We went up to Dr. Halbert Gulbrandson, as our regular doctor was not available. Six or seven stitches closed the wound.

Mom's warning was partly right. The barbed-wire encounter did result in a noticeable lifelong scar on my chin (it became one of my identifying marks in the Army). But though I worried all the time, when I got old enough to shave I had no trouble. Dad was always nicking his face with his straight razor, but I used an electric shaver and that took care of that.

This whole saga was just another stepping stone to growing up.

Going to Town

To us curious little boys, going to town was always an adventure. In town there were stores with toys we had never heard about before and sidewalks made of smooth concrete, something never used on the farm. My mother never allowed Dad to pour a sidewalk, although I know he would have, as a convenience for her and the family. She said, "Sidewalks are for city folks, but we are country, and grass is plenty good enough."

Any chance we got, we begged to go to town with Dad. He had purchased a new GMC pickup in 1936 and it was beautiful, with a lot of chrome, a shiny green body and black fenders. We loved to ride in it.

Going to town with
Dad. Look out!
Here we come!

Charley Parker, who had a hardware store, was a good friend of my dad's and we always stopped there to pass the time of day. Charley sold coaster wagons and he had one in his window that would be the answer to any boy's dreams. I believe the brand was Rocket. It was light green with a black handle and shiny hubcaps. Every time I saw it in the window I absolutely worshiped it. Dad was not too interested because it was high-priced. The price tag said four dollars. I didn't give up, though, and still adored the wagon.

One day about the middle of summer we went into Parker's store and Charley told my dad, "That kid has been wanting that wagon for so long, I think he should have it. I can let it go for three dollars and still come out."

Dad said, "You have a deal!"

Fred and I got the wagon down and were out the door in a flash. We had looked over those cement sidewalks, which seemed to go downhill, and we couldn't wait to try out my new wagon. Away we went down the sidewalk like a shot. People had to hurry to get out of our way. We went all the way around the block and as we sped around the corner by the dimestore we turned sharp and ran right into a lady who was standing there. We hit her right in her shin bones. She got quite mad, shook her fist at us and said in a gruff voice, "You young whipper-snappers! I have a notion to pull down your britches and tan your hides!"

We saw that apologizing wouldn't do any good, so we pushed off and went down the street again toward the bank. The lady couldn't run fast enough to catch us. This new wagon was a deluxe model with roller bearings in the wheels and it really went fast. By now both Dad and his friend Charley Parker were running down the street to catch us before we ran somebody clean over.

Once the wagon got home, it lived a more relaxed life. We hauled puppies in it and a lot of kittens. After it got older and began to rust, we let Dad haul up to two full cans of milk in the barn. Wow, what a strong tough wagon! Those full cans weighed almost a hundred pounds each!

Jens Vigdahl had a neat grocery store just south of the Temple Theatre. Outside the store was a fake ice cream cone about three feet high. I knew it was metal and painted to look like ice cream. After the wagon adventure, when we all walked down the street the folks always held tight to our little hands so we couldn't escape and get in trouble. Fred would reach out as far as he could stretch as we went by the ice cream cone, to try to get a taste. One day he got loose and ran over to take a lick. Of course it wasn't ice cream at all, just painted on. He almost bawled and was so disappointed, Dad said, "Let's go down to the dairy and get some ice cream."

We had never been to the Viroqua Dairy before, so it was a super treat! Located just off Main Street, this popular dairy had ice cream cones, ice cream sundaes, malted milk and a music machine where you put in a coin and just like magic it began to play. After that if we insisted hard enough, we could always convince our folks to stop at the dairy.

I will always remember Jens Vigdahl and his grocery store. It wasn't like the stores you see today, but more like the stores in Norway. Jens specialized in items that our Norwegian immigrant community remembered from the old country. One of Jens's specialties was lutefisk (pronounced "loo-tah-fisk"). To those of you who are unfamiliar with lutefisk, it is codfish caught in the North Sea in an area famous for this kind of fish ever since the days of the Vikings. After the fish are caught and cleaned, they are put in racks and dried in the cold dry air. After several months they are as hard as a board, totally preserved and will keep for years. It is claimed that there is lutefisk in Norway more than three hundred years old that is still good to eat.

To prepare for eating, it has to be soaked in a lye solution for many days and then rinsed for as many days in a sack in the river. Jens received his lutefisk from Norway in wooden barrels in a lye-water solution. He had a very good business in this smelly fish. One season he sold 16,000 pounds. Even now, one hundred sixty years after Norwegians came to Wisconsin from the much loved homeland, lutefisk suppers are still held in area churches.

51

The menu will include lutefisk, meatballs, mashed potatoes and gravy, rutabaga, creamed peas, fruit salad, pickled herring, bread and butter, and lefse ("leff-sah," a flatbread made with potatoes). There are many side specialties that vary from community to community. Non-Norwegians may attend these suppers out of curiosity, cautiously taste the foods and find them good to eat, but they cannot identify what they are.

After eating more than twice what you thought possible, the ladies, all in Norwegian costume, appear with large trays piled high with desserts. These include specialty baking of unknown identity, unless you are Norsk. Maybe ten or twelve different varieties, but the whole meal is built around lutefisk. A true Norwegian dreams about these suppers all year and then gorges on those ethnic specialities.

More lutefisk is eaten in Wisconsin and Minnesota than in all of Norway. People in Norway say, "We don't have to eat that crap, because we have had refrigeration for over seventy years."

Jens's other specialty was pickled herring. Englishmen and other people who are not ethnically connected to Norway cannot stand the smell of our specialty fish, but we feel that they are the losers and we will eat herring and lutefisk just the same.

Saturday night used to be shopping night in Viroqua. The stores were open until at least nine o'clock. Young people came to town to meet others and to go to dances. Our parents did not like their children to be exposed to what went on in town on Saturday night. Viroqua was a wide open town with many saloons and other places of questionable moral character, so we very seldom were exposed to these so-called sinful carryings-on.

I remember one time when we did go, though, and Dad treated each of us kids to a bottle of soda pop. We sat in the car and drank it slowly to make it last as long as possible. I believe I had a bottle of orange pop. We were playing around and when I stuck my thumb in the bottle, it got stuck. I tried and tried, but it just wouldn't come out. Now my thumb started to swell and hurt. When Dad came to the car he found a very scared little boy.

I thought my thumb might come off, but Dad assured me that everything would be okay.

We were parked right in front of the Overbo and Hanson Shoe Store. These two businessmen were kind of connected to our family. Ingvar Overbo had come to our place when he arrived from Norway. In fact, my grandfather Ole T. Fortney sponsored him as an immigrant. He learned to speak English and studied under Ole T. to get American citizenship. Kenneth Hanson was born and raised about one-and-a-half miles from our home and was just about family, too. My dad said, "We will go in their store and find a way to get your finger free from that old bottle."

Kenneth Hanson tried to put some soap on my finger and work it out, but it was so swollen that that didn't work. He said, "I have a small hammer that will work."

We went downstairs in the shoe store and he sat me down by a little anvil that the shoemaker used to build and repair shoes and boots and carefully tapped on the bottle until it broke. Then all that was left was the neck of the bottle. I remembered someone talking about a bottleneck and now I knew what they were meant—a tight place where you couldn't get loose without help. He now very carefully tapped on the "bottleneck" until it broke and I was free. We wasted a good bottle, though, which was worth one penny. If you turned in five empty bottles, you could pay for another bottle of pop.

Living and Loving the Animals: Cows

When you grow up on a dairy farm, animals are part of your life and you just accept them. We boys went to the barn at chore time from our earliest remembrance, probably starting for me when I was three years old. I easily remember before we had a milking machine. It was in 1936 that my dad purchased used milkers from Sam Solverson. A milker consisted of a used pump and units; the brand was Perfection. These units were almost antique way back then, but they worked well. Some cows didn't like them, though, and almost jumped out of their skins when they heard or saw them. Those cows had to be milked by hand.

Feeding our calves

All our cows had names, as well as all the calves and the rest of the young stock. This made them part of an extended family. If a cow had to be sold it was a sad day and we kids would cry because we knew we would never see her again. We thought the sold cows just moved someplace else. We weren't told that they were butchered and eaten up by people. We knew that steers were butchered, but that was different. That was what steers were for, because they didn't give milk.

When cows go to the pasture in the spring they run and play and eat lots of grass. They also keep checking the fences to find weak spots where they might get out. It seemed like it was a running game with them to get through the fence. We had an orchard north of the house with fruit trees and some odd growing things that nobody liked, at least we kids, like horseradish and such. The grass grew lush and thick around the apple trees. Mother had her clotheslines between the rows of trees. About every ten days, the grass was tall enough to keep the cows satisfied for about one day. When we went after the cows one morning we opened the gate to the orchard. We did not know Mom had decided to wash clothes early that morning.

Mom was an early-in-the-morning person and had the wash finished and hung on the line before breakfast without noticing the open gate. After milking, as we came into the house for breakfast, we heard a terrible commotion down in the orchard with a lot of yelling and screaming. When the cow herd had headed back to the pasture after milking, the lead cow, named Sally Sue, spied the open gate and with a war whoop, headed for the orchard with all the other cows, tails in the air, right behind her.

It wouldn't have been so bad if they had just peaceably eaten grass, but they headed right for Mom's clean wash. These cows, which were normally quiet, docile and ladylike, were running head first into white sheets that Mom had carefully bleached and hung on the lines with care. Some cows were running about with parts of ripped sheets hanging from their heads, all having a gay old time. Other cows were pulling overalls off the line and walking on them. Mother was yelling and screaming at the cows and swatting them with her broom. She was also crying and I believe I even heard a few swear words. Ma never ever swore, so she must have been very upset.

We now had to try to remedy this terrible situation. Dad was an easy-going sort of man who never got angry or ever swore. He always said, "If you hold your temper and count to fifty before you say anything, the situation may look much better. If you are still upset, count to fifty again." I have followed Dad's advice over the years and it works.

The first thing that had to be done was to get rid of those wild cows. If we had started yelling and screaming and pounding them with sticks we may never have gotten them out of the orchard. Dad walked slowly through the herd and talked to the cows. He then walked slowly over to the gate without looking back and then, in a pleasant voice, began calling the cows. They all started to go toward him. When the last one left the orchard he said, "You can shut the gate now, boys."

Our next challenge was a very irate mother who was weeping over her ruined laundry. Dad consoled her and told her to sit down and relax and enjoy the birds and the beautiful blossoms on the trees. The Jasperson family where Mom grew up didn't operate like this. They sometimes stayed mad for weeks and everybody had hurt feelings. While she was cooling down we helped Dad pick up the pieces of ruined sheets and towels. The overalls weren't really hurt and we just hung them up again.

Dad said, "It wasn't as bad as all that, was it? Come in the house and we will eat some breakfast."

Mom was still upset, but she finally stopped shaking and combed her hair and put on a fresh apron. We saw that she was starting to cool down. After breakfast Dad said, "You know, those sheets and towels were getting awfully thin and some were patched. Let's put on fresh clothes and all go uptown in the old Plymouth and then go to the Felix Store and buy some new sheets and towels. We need to grocery shop anyway. Jens Vigdahl's store is just up the street and Dahl's Drugstore has delicious ice cold root beer."

Dad had a way of turning a disaster into a perfect day. Mom had fun putting new sheets on all the beds. The cows forgot all about their adventure and everybody was happy. Dad did tell us boys, though, "Don't let that happen again. We may not be able to talk our way out of it the next time."

Horses

Fred and I entered life during a transition era on Wisconsin farms. We did not realize it at the time, but it was real and far-reaching. This big change was the phasing out of horses and their replacement with motor vehicles and tractors. Dad had a tractor even before we were born, but it was used only for plowing and smoothing down the ground before planting. When I was seven years old, he purchased his first new tractor, an F-20 Farmall. The dealer in Viroqua drove it out from town one morning and I still remember the day when that new shiny red machine drove in the yard. I remember the price, too—$900 and four horses.

Dad's new tractor, a red 1939 IHC F-20 Farmall. We still have it.

The dealer, John Stewart, took horses in trade, since there were many old farmers who weren't about to part with horses and buy one of those newfangled smelly tractors. We still kept our team, though, Bob and Queen. Dad had owned them for about twenty years and they deserved a comfortable retirement on the farm. After all, this was their home, where they had lived all their lives. They could still do some light work like pulling the tobacco planter and cultivator and the hay mower. I look back now and marvel at how smart they were. If you said, "Get up a step," they would move ahead one step and then stop. When we harvested tobacco they would pull the tobacco rack and you would just talk to them and they would move ahead while you loaded or unloaded. And you could trust them with your life.

A stupid tractor was another story. You could yell at it all day long and it would never move unless you cranked it and got on and drove it ahead. Bob and Queen were a team and actually did teamwork with us. If you stopped a tractor on a slope and forgot to lock the brakes, it might roll away and roll down over a bluff, hit a tree and be a total wreck. Horses never did anything dumb like that. Almost everybody who grew up on these hillside farms can remember horror stories about tractor runaways that ended with death for a farmer or one of his children. So sad.

One end of our barn was the horse barn. When Grandfather built the barn in 1909 he built harness hangers in the wall. These were pieces of a "wagon tire." What is a wagon tire? If you study an antique farm wagon that has wooden wheels you will see that the outside rim of this wheel is steel. Wagons lasted people a long time and eventually this steel band would wear out and need to be replaced. Grandfather was a blacksmith and fixed everything himself. He of course saved the old steel band from the wagon to use for something else. He would heat it up in his forge and bend it into the right shape for a harness hanger and when the masons built the barn wall they put these hangers in the cement in just the right places. Now, after a hundred years, these hangers are still there and can still be used. They were a good use for scrap iron.

You may ask, how did they put a new rim on the wooden wagon wheel? Grandfather bought new flat steel stock and bent it in a circle, then hammer-welded the ends together and put it on the wheel. It was not as simple as that; the steel had to be very tight or it might fall off. He made a circle out of this new steel, but made it just a little smaller than the wooden part. Then he heated it in his forge until it was almost red-hot. Heat made it expand enough so that it would just slip over the wood. He then poured water over it to cool it before the wooden wheel caught fire. The steel shrank and got real tight around the wood.

The last process was to use a weird tool he had in his shop called a tire shrinker. I never saw it used because it was obsolete before I was born. It had a long handle to operate a kind of pincers to crimp the "tire" onto the wood. No one would have the patience or know-how to do this today. Even the Amish farmers don't use this kind of wagon wheel.

The horses all had names and personalities. Our team of course was Bob and Queen. They were jet black, but Bob had a small white spot on his forehead. When Dad went threshing he always took Bob and Queen hooked to the wagon with the "basket rack." A basket rack is one that has sides as well as ends. When you haul grain bundles, the side racks keep the bundles from falling off. A basket rack is just a memory from the past since threshing machines have been replaced by combines now for many generations.

Dad had painted the wagon rack white, probably because there was some white paint left over from painting the house. The wagon wheels were painted red. The horses' harnesses were well oiled and had shiny studs on the leather straps. Dad wore a white shirt with the cuff turned up two turns. He had a straw hat, not the ordinary floppy kind like most farmers wore, but a dress hat, white in color. When he drove down the driveway we were very proud of him and his rig. A lot of farmers who had no pride would have a rig just patched together, unpainted, on a rusty wagon with junky wheels. They would wear ragged dirty shirts and patched overalls. My mother would think to herself, how disgusting!

The four horses that were traded off for the tractor were first, Jack, an old riding horse, and second, Belle, a female Belgian that was "green broke," just learning how to be driven. The last two were Prince and Princess, both offspring of Queen. They were young and not yet "broke to drive." These four did not have personalities like Bob and Queen, so we kids were not as much attached to them.

The ultimate insult was to accuse someone of being a horse thief. This perception would carry over to the next generation ("He comes from a family of horse thieves"). Even if a family member moved to town and opened up a business, the stigma was still there. If his grandfather may have been a horse thief, you could not trust this man either, because he might not be honest. Horse ownership was strictly on sacred ground.

A mule is a hybrid animal, a cross between a male donkey and a female horse. Mules are very strong and good workers, but many farmers wouldn't own one because if you drove mules you were considered a lower class person. This stigma is hard to outgrow. In the Amish community, no one owns a mule. It is against their religion to cross races. Among their people, young people cannot marry Jews, Orientals, Negroes or Indians, or anyone from a different race. Their teaching strictly forbids it and it would be an unpardonable sin. Your soul would be condemned to hell. They feel the same way about their animals, whether it be their horses (no mules—they are a different race from horses). No cattle crosses—Holstein cow with Jersey bull, etc.). Most "Englishmen" do not agree with them.

A man who beats his horse is just as evil as the man who beats his wife. I heard about a man who was always mean to his horses and even pinched them with pliers. But horses don't forget and if they get a chance they will get even. This abused horse finally saw his chance. He bit the owner on the shoulder, picked him up with his teeth and shook him until he saw stars. He then threw him over his head and he landed head first in the manure pile! Horse had gotten his revenge and was now even.

Tales from Hinkst School

Walking to School

In my youth, going to school was a very important part of my day. From home to the Hinkst School, if you went by the road, was one-and-a-quarter miles, but if you took a shortcut through the woods, it was probably three-fourths of a mile. This way was known as the "woods way," while the other route was known as the "road way." Of course if it was raining, my dad drove us to school in the family car. But normally we walked.

In the winter time we rode our sleds on the road. We started right by our house, slid down the icy road, and got to school in about eight minutes. The last hill, Hinkst Hill, with the one-room school house right at the bottom, was probably the most dangerous. You would go downhill so fast that your eyes would water and meeting a car could result in tragedy. Luckily there wasn't much traffic on the roads back then and we seldom saw a car. One time, however, Frederick Dregne slid down the Hinkst Hill during noon hour and a car driven by Harold Dregne met him at the bottom of the hill. Harold slammed on his brakes and Frederick dragged his feet trying to stop, but slid right under the stopped car. Nobody was hurt, but everyone who saw this near disaster was scared. Our teacher laid down the law—Nobody was allowed to slide down this hill ever again! The following year we had a new teacher who had not heard about this close call and we slid down our hill in the middle of the road again.

The Woods Way

Walking alone through the woods was a scary experience for a six-year-old child. We followed a path that appeared to have been the remains of an old wagon road. None of my old maps show a road through those woods, but there may have been one anyway. Oftentimes the early settlers had alternate routes that they traveled for some reason or other. This path of ours went into the woods on the Lewison 40, then across the Traastad 20, then came out on open land owned at that time by Peter Johnson. From there it was just a short distance down the hill to the Hinkst School.

This path was well used over the years, since my father and his brothers and sisters and cousins had all walked to school on the same route. In the winter when the snow was deep, my Grandfather Ole T. Fortney would hitch a horse to a log and plow the path for his children to walk to school on. Back then it was not uncommon to see wolf tracks on their school path. Wolves liked the smooth path because it was easier walking.

To a small child whose imagination runs wild there can be many scary things in the woods. My classmate Carter Thompson and I did our best to be brave, but we still imagined lions and tigers and bears lurking through the trees, just waiting for a chance to grab a little boy and eat him alive. The big boys made us walk way ahead of them and made fun of us for being such scaredy-cats.

The Hollow Stump

By second grade we were much braver, and curious about our surroundings. Along the path through the wood there was a large hollow stump and one afternoon on the way home we investigated it. Lo and behold, hidden in the stump was a pack of cigarettes and some matches. Evidently when the big boys, both eighth graders, made us walk so far ahead, they were stopping to have a smoke! Our evil little minds thought, if they could do that, why not us, too? We each took a cigarette and lit it. As it was the first time for both of us, and we were only seven years old, we were not ready for the results. The smoke was so strong we almost strangled and when we stood up to go home we were so dizzy, we could barely stand up!

The Wasp's Nest

One time on the way to school in the morning we spied a large paper wasp's nest on a low branch of a tree. We decided it would be nice if we surprised our teacher, since we were studying nature. The nest appeared empty so we carefully broke the branch and hurried to school. Teacher was enthralled with this masterpiece of nature and thanked us over and over. She then fastened the nest to the wall right above the bookcase. We felt very proud of our great find. By about 10:15 in the morning, the nest had warmed up and a strange buzzing sound came from above the bookcase. To our horror, black wasps started coming out of the nest. With a blood-curdling scream the teacher grabbed the nest and threw it into the furnace. And that was not only the end of the paper wasp's nest, but teacher would not speak to us for the rest of the day.

The Grave

One night going home from school, near the path where we entered the woods, we saw a large hole dug in the ground. We had no idea what it was for. The next night we found out: A large gray horse was lying dead right next to the hole. One of Peter Johnson's horses had taken ill. As the horse was very old, Peter led him over to the hole and shot him, thereby putting him out of his misery. This was often done with an old horse. If you sold him to a horse dealer, you would never know what happened to him. He might be resold to someone who had no mercy and your trusty friend might suffer for a long time, until he starved to death or died in harness.

When a horse has been your friend for up to thirty-five years, you get very attached to him, and it becomes a man's duty to put him away without any suffering. The old Norwegians had very low opinions of people who let horses or any other animals lie around and suffer until they finally died.

When horses get old, their teeth wear out. They can get along during the summer when they can eat soft grass, but when winter comes and all they have to eat is dry hay, they practically starve to death because they cannot chew the hay or digest it.

Oftentimes putting down a horse is planned many months in advance. Since they can get along quite well on soft grass and in late fall their coat is in prime condition, the Norwegian farmer would plan ahead for the fateful day in the fall of the year. After killing the horse, he would skin him and the hide would be tanned and finished as a beautiful robe. We have a robe that is our memory of my dad's riding horse, Francie. Francie was put down in 1926. Her hide, the robe, was used over the next eighty years for many things, such as a lap robe when going to town with a team and bobsled. It has kept many kids warm on sub-zero winter nights. It was used to cover the radiator on early automobiles to protect them from freezing. Leather mittens were made from the hide of the horse's legs. These mittens had long gauntlets that reached almost to your elbows. Grandmother would knit wool liners for your mittens.

The horse that has been part of your life continues to be part of your memories until Our Lord summons you to come home to eternity.

A Mysterious School Lesson

Our teacher in first and second grade was a good looking young lady named Irene. She had her own car, a Chevrolet. She also liked the boys, including the eighth grade boys in our school, who were fourteen years old. Oftentimes she would let them drive her car to their homes and then she would go home from there.

Some things went on in school that we little children did not understand until many years later. One day we went outside for morning recess, but one eighth grade boy stayed inside with the teacher. When recess was over we could not get back inside. The door was locked and the shades were all pulled down. Eventually noontime came and the door was still locked. We little children were getting hungry and could not understand what was happening. Finally at about one o'clock the door opened. The schoolroom smelled of cigarette smoke and the teacher and the eighth grade boy both looked like "the cat that ate the canary."

Many years later we put two and two together and decided that this had been a lesson in carnal knowledge! Irene had relationships with several boys in our school as well as young men in the community. If the school board or parents had found out, she would have been fired. If this had happened today she would have gone to jail. She taught at our school for only two years.

Playing in the Creek

We had many narrow escapes on the creek that was right behind the school. One time in the spring when the creek was flooding, the big boys dared me to jump on a big piece of floating ice and go for a ride. I did not want to be called a sissy so I did and that was a mistake! The ice sheet started to break up and as it got smaller it started to sink. By this time I was almost halfway down to the stone quarry. The big boys now were getting concerned because this whole adventure was their idea. They ran along the bank and pleaded with me to jump off, which I did. By that time the floodwater was almost to the top of my overshoes, so I had no choice. The big boys made me promise that I would <u>never</u> tell the teacher or anyone else because they knew they would get in deep trouble. I stuck by my promise and never told anyone.

There are a multitude of other tales of Hinkst Hollow adventures, but we will save them for another day.

Funerals

Small children are very impressionable and we Fortney kids were no exception. When we were allowed to go along to a funeral for a relative who had passed away, Mother explained to us that all people die eventually and their souls ascend to heaven to be joined with others that have gone on before them. We may miss the person who has just died, but on the day of the funeral, we celebrate his or her reunion with the Lord.

The body is buried in the grave to return to the earth. Mother quoted the Bible verse, "From dust ye come and to dust ye shall return." Our folks showed us the graves in the cemetery where our ancestors were buried. We asked Mother if she would be buried there someday, too, and she told us, "Yes, also Dad, and someday you kids will be buried here, too." This whole story impressed us so much that we could hardly wait for Sunday so we could attend church and Sunday School again.

Dressed for church.
Fred and I both
hated short pants.

After the funeral we went to the home of the person who had died and the house was filled with relatives, some of whom had traveled hundreds of miles for this special day. When we got home afterward we thought about what we had learned that day. The next day we thought some more and started to wonder about the little animals we saw around us. What happened to them when they died? We saw cats eating birds all the time and dogs that had been run over by cars lying dead along the road. What about them?

We decided to do something about this problem. We would have funerals for the little animals and maybe they could go to heaven, too. Between the machine shed and the old house, there was a space about thirty feet long and twelve feet wide that served no useful purpose. This would be our cemetery. There was a pile of bricks there, too, which would make perfect monuments. I would be the gravedigger, Fred would be the preacher and give the sermon, Sue and David would be the congregation and sing songs. If we looked around we could find something to have a funeral for. We would make a box for a casket and pick flowers down on the lawn in Mom's flower garden to put on the graves.

We went looking for a customer and found one almost right away. A baby robin had fallen out of a nest and died. Our first funeral was a success! We then served imaginary lunch of mud pies and imaginary coffee. After the burial we went looking for another victim and found a dead cat. Fred preached a good sermon in imaginary Norwegian. Very impressive! We didn't have time to make another casket so we went down to the house and raided Mom's rag bag and found a whole bunch of old socks that the men had discarded. These would serve just as well for a casket and the body might go from dust to dust a little faster.

This adventure was so successful, we decided that to do it right, we needed a church. The old house was right there, so why not? There would be plenty of room for imaginary relatives who would come from afar. We had had two funerals the first day and needed another customer. After each funeral we took a brick and stood it on end to mark the grave. We went looking and found a half eaten rabbit that an evil tomcat had killed. We were horrified to think that this may have been the Easter Bunny. This was a sad funeral because bunny had been murdered and we knew that tomcat would go to hell!

The next day we looked and looked, but could not find a body. At this time Mother and Aunt Mary knew nothing about what we were doing. They should have been suspicious, though, because we kids were too quiet. I have heard that if children get too quiet, they might be up to no good. We wanted another funeral, but there were no customers. I think there is a little bit of evil lurking in the back of the minds of all people and even children are not exempt.

I remembered seeing two steel traps hanging on the wall in the shop and seeing a lot of sparrows going in and out of the window in the hog house. Here comes that evil streak. We took these traps and set them and placed them right in the window of the hog house. In about fifteen minutes we had two dead sparrows in the traps. We removed them and reset the traps. We were back in the funeral business! We then conducted our first double funeral.

We had many funerals every day because we caught as many sparrows as we needed. By now Mom and Aunt Mary started to get suspicious because we spent so much time up around the old house. When Mom figured out what we had been doing she just about hit the ceiling. We got a sermon on causing harm to God's little creatures that were innocent of doing anybody harm, and how we should feel sorry for the evil that we were doing. "Just think of all the baby sparrows that are now starving to death because of you." We had never thought about it that way. Mom said we should pray to God and ask forgiveness for our sins and promise Him never ever to do this again.

We had been put back on the path of the straight and narrow. Our funeral business was now on hold, but the option was still open for burying legal customers. We put the traps back up on the wall in the shop.

The Old House

The old house mentioned in the "Funerals" chapter is the house Father and his family lived in before his own father built the new house in 1917. It was located just below the new house on the same lawn. My Grandfather Ole T. Fortney's plan, when he built the new house, was either to tear down or move the old house, since it detracted from the view of the new construction. I don't have any exact information of what was discussed, but eventually they decided to move it and use it for something else.

Getting ready to move the old house

I heard stories about the day it was moved. The house had no basement so the men just jacked it up and put a couple of skids underneath. Most likely the skids were cut in the woods. With skids the house would slide better. Grandfather Ole T. had at least three teams of horses and all the neighbors were willing to bring their horses over, too. There were probably eight or nine teams. Somehow all the teams hooked onto the house and when the chains tightened up, the horses laid into their harnesses and pulled. The house started to move and they kept right on going. If the horses had stopped, they wouldn't have been able to start again.

Ole T. and his sons hadn't really decided where they were going to put the house, but something had to be decided real soon. Ole T. said, "Let's just park it between the tobacco shed and the machine shed, then go down to the house and have coffee. It is after three o'clock anyway. The horses need a rest. See how sweaty they are?"

So that is what they did. Karn had baked a cake and an apple pie or two on her new stove in the new house and there was fresh bread and your choice of cheese, sorghum molasses, honey, blackberry jam and premost. Karn made sure nobody went hungry. All the men visited and commented on the house moving project, then had more fresh bread and jam, and another piece of cake and pie, and more coffee, and more visiting.

Finally someone looked at the clock and saw that it was already after five o'clock and about chore time. Ole T. and the boys still hadn't decided where to park the house. Someone said, "It doesn't look too bad right where it's at," so there it stayed. Ole T. said to his sons, "If we make a big door in the south end wall, the house can be used for a shop for you boys to tinker on your cars, and we can strip tobacco in there, too. Just build a new chimney so a little stove can be hooked up."

This was back in 1917. Now we will fast forward to when Fred and I were growing up. We looked over the old house. There were many layers of wallpaper on the walls and under the wallpaper was newspaper printed in Norwegian. We had never been upstairs in the old house. There wasn't a stairway anymore, but if we looked from different angles, we could see things that fired up our curiosity and we just had to find a way to get up there.

One day Fred and I decided that maybe we could make some kind of ladder to get upstairs. Dad's big ladder was so heavy that we couldn't lift it. We found some boards and nails and proceeded to make a crude contraption to climb on. It was pretty rickety, but we could finally get upstairs. There was junk and pigeon poop everywhere, an old cabinet with pottery jugs inside, and in the large room was an antique foot-powered turning lathe. Now, you know about curious little boys. We figured out how to make that old lathe turn by pumping the foot pedal. We also discovered a trap door that went to the attic and up we went. I don't know what we expected to find, but we did find an animal skeleton back by the eaves. I am now sure that it was just an old tomcat, but at the time we were sure it was a wildcat.

Mom heard about our house adventure and told us in so many words, "Stay out of there! There are naily boards and broken glass to get hurt on and all that pigeon poop is full of germs and you will get sick and you could even die." We promised faithfully to stay out of there forever after, but when nobody was around, where do you think we went? You guessed it.

This is the same old house that was next to our animal cemetery.

In back of the old house was a kind of junk yard containing some old pieces of machinery and the remains of several old buggies that people used before they had cars. Some had been pretty fancy in their day, such as a two-seater with mohair seats and tops and gas lights. One was the buggy that Uncle Arthur came home from Missouri with. We discovered that if you tried hard enough you could get the wheels to turn. Then someone said, "Why not strip the buggy down and make a racer?"

We took everything off except the wheels and the center reach pole. The wheels would come off so we could polish up the axles and put on new grease. Next was to wire on a board along the center and find a way to steer. Two pieces of rope tied out near the wheels of the front axle was the answer. Now to try the buggy out. We went down the driveway and to the right. It went real fast, probably faster than any horse ever pulled it when it was new!

A bunch of cousins was visiting so we took our racer up the hill toward Uncle Malvin's house. There was room on our sitting board for at least six or seven kids. The heavier the load the faster it went, right down the big hill toward home. We didn't worry about cars or trucks coming. They would have to look out for themselves because we didn't have brakes. One problem we hadn't counted on: These old buggies had sat in the weeds so long, the spokes in the wheels where they had sat next to the ground were rotten enough so that when we went flying down the hill they would fly out until the wheel fell apart and we crash-landed. Back to the junk yard we went, to take a wheel off one of the other old buggies.

Over the length of one summer we used up all the wheels. Now what would we do? Maybe we could put our buggy together again and reinforce it with a piece of board. That didn't work worth a hoot, but school was about to start again anyway, so we gave up the buggy idea for the meantime. By the next spring our interests turned to other things and the buggy episode was all forgotten.

The new house Grandfather Ole T. Fortney built in 1917

The New House

For many years my grandparents dreamed of having a new house on the farm. Ole T. and Karn Fortney had lived in two other houses, where their children were born, but Karn dreamed of a large home where she and Ole T. could entertain guests, and since they lived on the home farm, they knew relatives would also visit regularly.

Ole T. looked to have a home as modern as the best homes in the city. Nordahl, one of his six sons, was in high school at this time and interested in architectural drawing and design. Ole T. and Karn told Nordahl what they wanted in a new house and Nordahl designed it to his parents' wishes. His first blueprint called for eleven rooms plus a breezeway and summer kitchen (a separate structure outside the main house). Ole T. studied the plan and said no.

"Summer kitchens are too old-fashioned," he told Nordahl. "Design a large kitchen on the west side of the house with two extra bedrooms above and an extra stairway up from the kitchen for hired help to get upstairs. Also design a screened-in porch off the kitchen to the south."

Karn said she wanted nine-foot ceilings downstairs, and eight-and-a-half foot ceilings upstairs. "Now, since we're having a back stairway for hired help, I want a formal carpeted front stairway for family and guests. An open upstairs porch will be good for airing out bedding and a place for the hired man to sleep when it gets hot. I also want a wide veranda on the front of the house where guests can sit on hot summer evenings and I can have plants to grow and enjoy."

Nordahl took these revisions and came up with an acceptable plan. The first floor included a long veranda, a spacious foyer with carpeted ascending stairs, a parlor off the veranda, a huge dining room, and a huge country kitchen measuring 16 x 16. Adjoining the kitchen were the pantry, a sitting room, and a large screened-in porch. Upstairs, a wide hallway ran the length of the house and off the hall were a bathroom and five bedrooms, four large and one small. There was an open porch off one of the large bedrooms. There was a laundry chute from attic to basement.

All told, the house had fourteen rooms, a big bathroom, a veranda at the front of the house, porches on first and second floors, and a full basement with 18-inch thick stone walls. Ole T. was a big man who wanted a big house for his big family. In our neighborhood, it was very unusual for anyone to build a house that big, but Ole T. knew what he wanted and needed, and he got it.

Today we use the sitting room off the kitchen as a TV and reading room, and the screened-in porch is now enclosed and serves as my office and writing room. The smaller bedroom upstairs is Jane's sewing room and we have one of the large bedrooms, but the other bedrooms are frequently occupied by visitors. In my grandparents' day, family members, guests and hired girls occupied the large bedrooms and the hired men shared the smaller bedroom. With all the company my grandparents had, there were times when as many as twenty-five people were staying in the house—and the house was kept in perfect order, with everyone pitching in to get meals on the table and to keep everything neat and clean.

Nordahl had come up with a good plan for his parents' new house. Meanwhile, watching the lumber market in 1916, Ole T. believed he saw a trend where lumber prices might go very high the following year. So, in the fall of 1916, he purchased all the lumber (southern yellow pine), flooring, and shingles that he would need for the new house, hauled it home that winter with horses and bobsleds, and stored it in the tobacco sheds. Early in 1917, lumber went from $6.50 per thousand feet to $13.00 per thousand. Ole T.'s hunch had been correct.

The stone for the 18-inch basement wall came from Gust Fortney's quarry about two miles from our farm. This stone was hauled in with horses in the fall of 1916, piled tightly together and covered with wet straw so it would not dry out. Stone that is kept damp, the way it comes out of the ground, is much easier to cut to size when laying up a wall.

In the late spring of 1917, with lumber, flooring, shingles and stone all accounted for, it was time to start building. Ole T. hired Louis Sylvester as the main carpenter. Louis and his crew had built a house for Ole Thompson next door in the summer of 1916. He was known as an excellent carpenter, and he was also a farmer who milked cows and raised tobacco.

Ole T. wanted electric lights, just like houses in town. He purchased a Delco Light Plant to be installed in the basement. It consisted of a generator powered by a small gasoline engine with an exhaust pipe running out through the rock wall. Twenty-one wet cell batteries provided 32 volts DC. The generator had to be run daily, every evening, to charge the batteries. Electricity was also wired into the barn. The house was wired with "tube and knob" wiring, which was quite heavy for the 32-volt system. The wiring is heavy enough for today's lighting systems. Updates, of course, include a 150 amp box and additional circuits for outlets and big appliances. The building process went smoothly and the house was finished in twelve weeks, which was fantastic when you remember that the builders had no power saws, drills or even cement mixers.

Two of Ole T.'s sons, Nordahl and Malvin, poured the basement floor in two days. They mixed all the concrete by hand in a mortar box and carried it down in five-gallon pails. The carpenters stayed at the site and slept under the trees. The top men got $1.50 per day and the others got $1.00 a day. Some of the neighbor boys came over to help and were very glad to earn seventy-five cents a day. They put in long days and worked from daylight until dark. Karn of course kept them all well fed.

Construction of the new house began May 22, 1917, and the family moved in November 29, 1917. Recently in the bottom of a drawer I found my Grandfather Ole T's account book, where he recorded all expenditures to the penny, and the total cost of building the new house was $4,506.09. In our area in 1917, a new home could be built for $1,000, though without electricity or running water. (It was not yet customary for farm houses to have electricity or indoor plumbing.) In fact, one particular house in our area, a good sized house, too, was built in 1917 for four loads of hay, two heifers and $200 cash.

A bathroom inside a farm home at that time was definitely a novelty, and the bathroom in Ole T. and Karn's house was spacious and modern. Located on the second floor, it measured 9 x 12 feet and had a large window that looked out onto the north lawn. The kitchen measured 16 x 16 and had a smaller room called a pantry, with built-in cupboards and work space, plus a stairway to the basement. In the basement, Karn wanted a laundry stove where she could boil clothes to get them extra clean.

When I was young, my father (Alfred, called Fred) told me, "Some day we will attempt to move that hated stove and if we can 'accidentally' drop it, we can legally haul it to the ditch." My dad believed that boiling clothes was not only unnecessary, but downright dangerous for the ladies of the house, and also for the children who were playing nearby. Many women and children were badly burned and scarred from accidents resulting from this dangerous practice of boiling clothes.

Many happy family gatherings were held in the new house. Former ministers from Franklin Church stayed at the house when on vacation. Teachers at Hinkst School roomed there. Ole T. sponsored young immigrants from Norway: The three Overbo brothers were there at one time or another; Sigvald Knutson and others spent their first year or so in America with Ole T. and Karn.

Ole T. suffered with ill health the last years of his life. He had typhoid fever, blood poisoning and diabetes, and spent the last year of his life in bed. My mother (Ruby) nursed Ole T. twenty-four hours a day. In December of 1935, Ole T. passed away, only eighteen years after he built his beautiful house. Karn passed away in May of 1939. She had planned to work in her flowerbeds the next day, but died of a stroke in the night.

The third generation now lives in Ole T.'s house and the fourth generation is planning for when they will take over.

Our Big Farm House:
Bursting with Life

Old houses have many stories and secrets in their past. Our house is about to start on the fourth and fifth generation of the same family and I will attempt to tell a few of the stories. I'm sure many more tales have been lost over the years and will never be told.

Ole T. Fortney, my grandfather, was a tall man and most of his six sons were six feet tall. His sons were Theodore, Carl, Arthur, Alfred, Nordahl and Malvin. (He had a daughter, Elisabeth, and two children who died in infancy.) Ole T. thought big and in 1917 built his house big to fit his large family, and anybody else that came along. We know there were two or three hired men here at times and one or two hired girls. The school teacher always stayed here, too. Just think of the food preparation for ten to fifteen adults, as well as young children. Tobacco harvesting crews also stayed here, and needed three meals a day plus coffee lunch twice a day.

We young kids kind of ran wild among all the grownups. There were mysteries about the house that puzzled us and our parents were very busy and did not have time to try to solve our problems. One mystery was the upstairs back hall. When you looked in the bathroom and then in the hallway, it seemed there must be a secret room in the wall, but no way to get to it. Was there something in there that children were not allowed to see? There also seemed to be a space between two walk-in closets that did not make sense. We never figured this out.

Another mystery was the dirty clothes chute. It went clear up to the attic and down to the basement, where dirty clothes fell into a large bin to wait for wash day. The mystery was that a favorite shirt or pants might disappear down this chute for five or six months and then reappear in the dirty clothes bin, and then something else would disappear the same way and show up weeks or months later.

This clothes chute thing bothered us. With our new flashlights we decided to look up the clothes chute and guess what? Right there, about halfway up, was my favorite blue pants hanging on a splinter in the boards. It would eventually get knocked off by more dirty clothes coming down. Mark one mystery solved.

The back stairway had one squeaky step, the very top step. Believe it or not, this step squeaked when the house was built in 1917 and today, in 2010, after ninety-three years, it still squeaks.

When my parents were first married, they went out one night to a party. When they came home, rather than turn on the lights and wake everybody, they came up the back stairs side by side, arm in arm, in the dark. When they reached the top, here comes Ole T., all excited and saying, "Where is Ruby? I only heard one squeak!" They had stepped on the top step together. Dad turned on the lights to prove to Ole T. that nothing bad had happened to Ruby.

When the school teacher stayed at the Ole T. Fortney house, she went out on dates, and knowing about the squeaky step, took off her shoes and tiptoed up the steps in the dark, so the hired men wouldn't know what time she got home. This was a good plan until she made one mistake. She hadn't counted the steps and one night, what she thought was the top step was the second from the top. She stepped over the second step, tripped on the top step and fell against the wall, then onto the floor. The hired men heard it all and had a good laugh. Norma was humiliated and didn't speak to those guys for a week.

The hired men tormented Norma. One night while she was out they found some blankets and towels and stuffed them inside a pair of men's overalls and a man's shirt and put it in her bed and tucked the blankets around it. When she sneaked in late that night she did not turn on any lights, undressed in the dark and crawled into bed. Alas! She thought there was a man in her bed! She let out a scream that would have awakened the dead. The hired men laughed and laughed and Norma would have killed them if she had had a chance. She did not miss them when the school year ended and she was able to go home for the summer.

Norma liked my Uncle Malvin, who wasn't married yet. Every day she dreamed of going out on a date with him, but he never noticed her. Besides, he had other girlfriends. One even helped him plan his new house. Malvin had house parties in the new house and invited his friends, but somehow he never remembered Norma. She would sit out on our front porch and listen to the dance music coming from next door. Years later, after Malvin had been married to Kay for many years, my mother had company here in the big house. Malvin and Kay were invited and so was Norma Neprud. Malvin was probably seventy-five years old by then and so was Norma. Now he noticed her and was talking and reliving old memories with her. Aunt Kay was absolutely fuming and looked daggers at Malvin and Norma.

Up in the Attic

The phrase "the attic" is used in our family like the name of your best friend. It is a page out of history for our family and has been used as much as the other fourteen rooms of our house. It is a place to store books, trunks and favorite memorabilia of days gone by. After you climb up the steep stairs, it is almost breathtaking to see the large area the attic covers. The ceiling is twelve feet high and the floor measures forty-eight feet long and thirty-two-and-one-half feet wide. There are three dormers built outwards and six windows to let in lots of light. Close to the chimney is a ladder that leads up to the deck on top of the roof. The floor is six-inch-wide pine boards that are covered with linoleum and old carpet that was much too good to throw out. The windows are washed each season and fresh curtains give it a homey look. The lady of the house for the last three generations has always said that an attic window without curtains looks like a house partly undressed.

Years ago when they raised their own seed corn, this was the best place to dry the cobs of corn. There were boards nailed to two-by-four uprights on three sides of the attic with nails driven through to secure the cobs of corn. If this had been attempted in any other building on the farm you would have problems with mice, rats and birds stealing the seed corn all the time.

When they butchered in the fall, the cured hams and bacon slabs were hung from the rafters. In the wintertime it was cold in the attic with good air circulation so the meat was well preserved. The womenfolk for three generations have always saved seed from their best flowers and garden crops and herbs. Where do they dry them? In the attic, of course.

The west end of the attic where there is no dormer has been the storage area for Christmas decorations and toys. They seem to multiply over the years so when you decide what to put up this year it is almost like going shopping in a store. There are decorations that were favorites many years ago when we were young. We have some decorations that are eighty years old and many "Made in Japan" from before the Second World War. Electric lights for the tree are a different story. If you read the fine print on the box they are only designed to last a short time. These we replace at least every two years, sometimes every year.

A fire on a Christmas tree can be a heartbreaking disaster. Kids always have some toys that they will never part with. There is plenty of space back under the eaves for piles of memories. Now that we have grandchildren, one of their biggest thrills is to go "up to the attic" and dig through toys that their dad or mom played with when they were their age many years ago. For some of them we saved the original boxes and stored them on shelves and they look like new yet. When we grew up we did not have many toys and they were worn out completely when we got done with them.

It is a natural thing to save pieces of the past and we have a family that has always saved favorite items. My grandparents and parents could read and write Norwegian. Their song books, Bibles, encyclopedias and magazines, all written in norsk, are still there for future generations to see and enjoy.

My father's World War I uniform, helmet, mess kit and canteen and souvenirs of France are in excellent condition. Old-fashioned beds and dressers have been reconditioned and used as furniture in guest rooms. Remnants of when the house was built are tucked back under the eaves or used as storage boxes. The old Victrola (a windup record player) has a special place as well as the large copper kettle and the party line hand-crank telephone. Torn quilts that were lovingly handmade by Grandmother Karn are dust covers over suitcases, hat boxes and baby furniture. A long line of clothes collected over several generations hang on hangers waiting to be used in high school plays and Sunday School programs. When our daughter, Nicky, got married many of these clothes were modeled at her wedding shower in a style review of past wedding dresses and attire. Such fun the guests had in remembering the memories and connections of each one.

When we were small I remember when a carpenter was hired to redo the screens and storm windows. After putting on new screening and repairing the frames he painted them all and they looked just like new. This was in the spring. After the repaired screens were put back in the house and the storm windows taken off, he repaired them by replacing some broken glass and re-putting where necessary and painting them. Now they were ready to put on next fall. Where was this all done? In the attic, of course. The attic had served as a carpenter shop that year.

When we grew up we played in the attic in the spring and fall. In the summertime it got so hot up there that you could hardly breathe. During the winter when it got down to twenty degrees below zero, I believe the temperature in the attic was nineteen below.

During the Second World War all boys played war. So did Fred and I. We had war games that came from the store, but if we let our imagination run wild, there was no limit. We played war up in the attic. There was a small pile of bricks up there that were left over from when the chimney was built. They would make perfect "block buster" bombs. The clothes chute that went to the basement also went up to the attic so cleaning rags and dirty curtains could be dropped down to be washed. We studied this out. Ah-ha! A perfect place to drop our bombs. We would drop them on the imaginary German soldiers that were hiding in Mom's dirty clothes bin in the basement. She didn't approve of this adventure at all and told us quite sternly, "Do not do this again ever!!" I suppose it was somewhat unnerving to hear bricks rattling through the wall all the way from the attic to the basement.

One spring when I was ten years old I was in the milk house with Dad one evening. He was rinsing out the milk cans and setting up the milkers. Our hired man at the time, Kenneth, came in the milk house with his hands in his pockets and said, kind of matter-of-factly, "Freddy, I just thought I should tell you your house is on fire." Dad at that time was forty-eight years old and in very good condition. He instantly sprang into action and grabbed two sixteen-quart milk pails, dipped them into the cooling tank and took off running to the house. The roof was on fire in one place, evidently from a hot spark from the furnace. It hadn't rained for some time and the cedar shingles were bone dry! He kicked the house door in, yelled, "House on fire!" and ran up the back stairs two and three steps at a time, then ran down the hall and up the attic stairs. He set down one pail and then threw the water from the other onto the fire where it by now had burned through the roof. He then climbed the ladder to the roof and dumped the other pail on the fire and luckily the fire went out.

Had he gotten up there ten minutes later it would have been too late and the house may have burned to the ground. Mom and Aunt Mary didn't realize what all the fuss was about until it was over. It was a close call.

Dad said, "We will let the fire in the furnace go out and not light it again unless it is raining. I will get Martin Berg from uptown to put a new fire resistant roof on this summer to protect our home."

When Martin and his crew came out, Dad decided to insulate the house too, plus put a new roof on the barn and also on one tobacco shed. He said, "Let's keep right on going and paint everything, too." They painted all the out-buildings bright red.

All these memories are connected to "up in the attic."

Hired Girls

Over the years we had many hired girls. Some of them didn't know a thing about housekeeping. The parents looked for a family that had a house with some modern conveniences and hired out their daughter hoping she would learn something and attract a young man to marry so they didn't have to support her anymore. My mother needed help with her large household and often ended up with these girls who came to us like a "blank slate." Most had never seen electric lights or a bathroom. Many had never seen running water inside a house. How could a young lady get to be sixteen years old and never have been taught how to peel potatoes or make a bed? My mother had a real challenge on her hands with some of these hired girls.

Some were willing to learn and did quite well. Others were an accident waiting to happen. One girl who was here for only three months broke every dish in a set of twelve place settings in less than a month. Another poured kerosene on an open fire in the cook stove and set the kitchen on fire. If Dad hadn't been able to move so fast we would have lost the house. There is a charred place on a leg of an antique table we are still using.

Fred and I were exposed to red measles by Katherine, a hired girl who had been gone for a week and a half. When she returned, she scooped us up and kissed us both on the mouth. The next day she came down with red measles. About twelve days later, Fred and I broke out in the same red spots. Wouldn't you know it was mid-December. We were quarantined and missed the Christmas program at school.

Katherine was working for us when Bernard Dregne worked here. Bernard was only seventeen years old then. Katherine had her eyes on Bernard and always found an excuse to go out the barn at chore time and hang around Bernard. He took my dad aside and said, "I am too young to get involved with a woman and I can't stand Katherine and wouldn't want her if she was the last female in the world. I am willing to pay her wages if you keep her out of the barn!" Dad thought this was kind of funny.

When Dad and Mom planned a trip to North Dakota to visit Dad's brothers who farmed out there, Dad told Bernard, "We will be gone for about two weeks and we will take my parents with us. I am leaving you to take care of the farm. Katherine will make meals and keep house for you."

Bernard said, "Oh, no, you can't trap me here with that predatory female."

Dad said, "Just be a gentleman and she can help you do the work."

Bernard thought it over and said, "Okay. There are two conditions. First, I am boss and what I say goes. Second, I want a key for the lock on my bedroom door so I can lock her out!"

While the folks were gone, Bernard did chores and hauled wood from the woods. He gave Katherine orders: "After I throw a load of wood through the window into the basement, you have to rank it up clear to the ceiling, starting from the other side of the basement. I'll be coming right back with another load, so if you are in the way, I'll cover you up with wood chunks."

Katherine piled wood almost every day for two weeks and she was so tired by night that she thought of nothing but sleep. Bernard took no chances, though. He locked his bedroom door every night, just in case.

When the folks got back from the North Dakota trip they were pleased to find the basement piled clean full of wood, enough to heat the house for more than a year. Katherine had sore muscles and blisters on her hands and was no longer speaking to Bernard. She had well earned her pay of $1.25 a week.

Another hired girl that I remember would "go into neutral" if Mother didn't watch her all the time. Her weakness was reading true romance books. One day Mother sent her outside to pick over peas and beans that she had picked that morning before the hired girl woke up. She instructed her, "While you are working with the peas and beans, you can watch the boys for me." As soon as Mother went back in the house the hired girl fished her true romance book out of her apron pocket and forgot everything else.

There was an antique gas engine over by the windmill that hadn't been used for many years and Fred and I decided to check it out. To us it looked like a barber chair. The open flywheels could be considered arm rests and the water reservoir was a seat. I would be the barber and Fred would be my first customer. He sat on the seat and I pretended to cut his hair. The open crankcase was right there and was full of a mixture of water, oil and grease. This would make perfect hair tonic! I took a double handful of this mess and rubbed it into Fred's hair. Then I applied some more for good measure. Next it was my turn for a haircut. Fred put a generous portion of "hair tonic" on my head and rubbed it in thoroughly. Just about then Mother looked out the door and her Jasperson temper exploded. She came flying out of the house. The hired girl didn't understand what all the fuss was about. She was so involved with her book that she had forgotten all about the peas and beans and Tom and Fred.

By the time Mother got through with her, she was crying. Dad, who had been working up by the shop, came down to see what all the fuss was about and Mother read him his pedigree, too. She said, "If you had gotten rid of that stupid old junk engine a long time ago, the boys wouldn't be such a greasy mess now!"

Dad didn't have an excuse so rather than irritate her more, he apologized and said, "Yes, dear, I'll take care of it right now."

In ten minutes, the old gas engine was gone. He backed the pickup truck up to it, hooked it up with a chain and pulled it in back of the tobacco shed. Fred and I would look it over every once in a while, but we never played barber again. We could still remember getting kerosene shampoo to clean our heads and having our clothes washed in the same smelly stuff.

I don't think that hired girl lasted much longer.

Bedbugs

I don't know who was the fussier housekeeper, Mother or Grandma Karn. It sure wasn't any hired girl. One morning Grandma was making the beds in the hired men's room. Normally she was quiet and even-tempered, but she let out a scream that everybody heard. She had found bedbugs in the beds! My mother heard her, came running and reacted the same way. My dad heard all the commotion and, thinking something horrible had happened, came running down to the house. He got there just as the women were rolling the mattresses off the upstairs porch. Pillows and sheets flew down next. Mom said, "Burn them! They're full of bedbugs!"

Dad didn't question them and did as he was told. When he came in the house later, he found Mom and Grandma mixing hot water and Lysol. Next they marched upstairs and scrubbed every inch of the hired men's room. While it was drying they threw the hired men's clothes out the window and then washed them in kerosene. By then the bedroom floor was dry, but they were not satisfied until they had revarnished it. Of course Dad had to drive to town and buy two new mattresses, and new pillows and sheets. The women told Dad to tell those filthy men to undress in the barn and take a kerosene bath. Then Dad was to give them clean clothes to wear, before they would be allowed to come in the house for supper.

This may have seemed like overkill, but it was the only time in ninety-three years that a bedbug was ever seen in this house.

Tom and Fred's 4-H chicken project

4-H Clubs: The Chicken Project

At age ten, you could join a 4-H club. This was a brand new experience. 4-H stands for Head, Heart, Hands and Health. The motto is "To make the best better" and the club slogan is "Learn by doing."

Our Aunt Leone Jasperson was the general leader of Belgium Builders 4-H Club, which she had organized some years before I was old enough to join. The club met in homes in the area. One person was elected president and he or she would conduct the meeting. We learned about parliamentary procedure, being attentive at meetings, and listening to the speaker for the night. We kids were now mixing with a whole new group of people.

The Belgium Ridge School was no longer used and we got permission to use it for a 4-H club house. Everybody rubbed and scrubbed until everything was clean; then we painted the inside in 4-H colors, green and white. We cleaned up the yard, mowed the lawn, and built an outdoor fireplace so we could cook hot dogs and such for our picnics. We were so proud of our accomplishments.

One night some kids from town came out to have a beer party, but Aunt Leone chased them away, telling them in no uncertain terms, "If this happens again, the sheriff will come out and he may treat you folks much more harshly." They never came back. These young people were quite ashamed of themselves because Aunt Leone knew some of them as well as their parents.

When we first joined 4-H we were supposed to take on just one project and do it well. Since we were growing up on farms, we were already familiar with the potential projects, such as calves, gardening and woodworking, and by the second year we wanted to take on many different projects. I took a calf the first year. The second year I took a calf and also chickens. Fred was now old enough to join and he also took chickens. We actually took them together. Mother kept track of all the expenses and, when our chickens began to lay eggs, the income. Fred and I now had our own income, other than an allowance. Mother said the chickens would have to pay back for the original cost and all the purchased feed. "The rest will be for you boys. Out of this income we will take money for your clothing and shoes and boots."

Somehow this did not seem fair, because we were planning on buying a lot of neat things that we saw in the stores. But Mother said, "These chickens are your business venture and we will treat it as such."

The new hens laid very well. Our three hundred hens laid up to 285 eggs per day and the gross income was more than twenty dollars a day. We were excited because we had never seen this much money before! The hens paid for themselves, paid for new clothes for school, paid for all the feed, and there was money left over. We were ready to go to town and spend it right away, but Mother said, "Not so fast! You have to save up for a rainy day. We will invest in war bonds and help our country and you will earn interest on your money."

We didn't quite understand what she told us, but knew she must be right. A twenty-five dollar war bond cost $18.50 and in seven years you could cash it in and get $25.

We thought our hens would keep on laying like this forever, but Dad said, "They are laying too good. Anytime chickens lay over 95% they are in a danger zone." Our hens were laying just at 95%. One day when we went to pick the eggs we found two dead hens. Their behinds were all bloody and their insides were gone. What in the world had happened to them? We ran up to the barn and told Dad. He said, "I was afraid of that. When hens lay too heavy, some hens will lay two eggs a day and sometimes even three. They have prolapsed oviducts and the other chickens see the red blood and chase those hens around and peck at their behinds until everything comes out and they die."

We thought this was just horrible and asked him what we could do. He said, "First we must change their feed so there is less protein, then put a red light in the hen house so the hens cannot see blood, and now for at least a week we will check the hens and if we see some that look bloody, we will butcher them and have chicken for supper."

This was a horrible setback for us little boys, but also a good learning experience. Our next shock came when Dad told us that chickens only laid steadily for about a year and then they went into a molt. They lost their feathers and grew new ones and when their feathers grew out, they would start laying again, but only about half as well as they did the first year. It didn't pay to keep hens more than two years. You had to grow another batch of chickens.

We asked, "What will happen to our chickens, then?"

Dad said, "We will sell them to Swift and Company and they will turn into Campbell's chicken soup."

This was a real shock to us, but also another learning experience on how the chicken industry worked.

The next spring we bought three hundred new chickens and started a new batch. That year the kind we got were DeKalb Hybrids. They were supposed to be good layers and quite calm, but I am afraid Dad was fed a line! Those chickens were flighty and nervous. The first problem started when the chickens were less than a month old. A darned cat got in the brooder house and did he make hay! After he killed six of the babies, the rest piled up in panic in a corner and about eighty of them smothered.

When they got bigger we let them go outside in the daytime, but locked them up at night. The brooder house was in the orchard where Mother had her clothesline. When night came the stupid chickens flew up in the apple trees to roost for the night and we had to chase them out of the trees and back into the house. If we didn't chase them in, they were targets for owls, which constantly stole chickens. Great horned owls are now protected, but when I was in high school in Future Farmers of America, you could earn an FFA letter for your sweater for shooting a great horned owl.

When fall came, it was time to empty the hen house and bring in the new pullets. We caught the old hens and took them to town to Swift and Company. Swift had an egg station where you could sell eggs and hens and roosters. The next thing was to clean the hen house real well so the new hens would not get any germs from the old ones. These wild flighty DeKalbs were hard to catch and we had to wear gloves so they didn't scratch us all up. We waited for these new birds to settle down, but they were so nervous that they were a real problem. When you opened the door they all flew up and hit the ceiling. If you moved fast they would hit the ceiling. We had to knock on the door, then open it slowly and walk in slow motion.

We thought maybe we would not have a problem with "blowouts" that year. Wrong. The last year was just a preview of things to come. These hens laid 98% to 100%. This was way up on the high side of the danger zone. Dad changed the feed, but it made no difference. Even with two red lights in the hen house, we found several dead hens almost every day. We found out that hogs liked dead chickens so we just opened a window and threw them out to them. After a couple of days when the hogs heard the window open they all came running to get a treat. Dad said, "I will make sure that we don't get any more chickens like those."

All the way through 4-H, Fred and I stayed with the chicken project. Our war bonds added up and I cashed mine in to buy a used car and Fred cashed his in to partly pay for a college education.

One year we sold eggs through Swift and Company to the Blackstone Hotel in Minneapolis, Minnesota. They were quite fussy. We couldn't wash the eggs; we had to use fine sandpaper to clean them. We had to candle the eggs to find and take out any that had weak shells or blood spots. Then we packed them carefully in the cases, small end down. We felt it was an honor to furnish eggs for a place as upscale and fancy as the Blackstone Hotel.

Another year we sold hatching eggs to Swift and Company. Their specialists came out and inspected the flock and gave us instructions and left roosters to breed the hens. We did not have DeKalb Hybrids anymore, thank goodness! We sure didn't want to be responsible for someone else getting those crazy chickens!

Outsiders

One warm sunny day in July 1944, a strange car drove up our driveway. It stopped out by the light pole and two ladies got out and walked toward the house. We kids were curious as to who they were and what they wanted. When they knocked, Mom went to the door with all of us behind her to meet these strangers. Always pleasant with strangers, Mom invited them in.

They introduced themselves. One was a lady Mom had met at a homemaker meeting, Edith Brevig, the county home economist. Edith introduced the other lady as Lois Hurley, a reporter from <u>Wisconsin Agriculturist</u> magazine. Edith and Lois told us they had heard from others about the Fortney family and wanted to meet us and interview us and possibly take some pictures. Mom was a little hesitant at first, but changed her mind and fully agreed to visit about her family.

She told about how Tommy and Fritz (Fred's nickname) had taken over washing the milking machine parts, strainers and pails. We had just started operating the milkers, too. We had three milkers, so Fred and I each ran one unit and Mom ran one, but Dad milked by hand, as some cows didn't like milking machines.

She told the story that around here, boys were very attached to the animals and if they sold a cow, they almost had to throw in a boy. Dad sold some cows one time without telling us boys about it. When we came home from school, we were so upset that he said, "After this, no cows can leave this farm until we talk it over with the boys first."

Fritz and I had also taken over the chicken flock. This was our first business venture, as told in the previous chapter.

We told Edith and Lois all about our chickens and how the money was used and saved up for special purposes later. They were very impressed with what we had been doing. Fred and I were now 4-H members in the Belgium Builders Club, where our Aunt Leone Jasperson was the general leader.

Lois Hurley took pictures of us kids, one of Fred holding one of his chickens and another of all four of us Fortney kids and our two Woolhiser cousins gathered around the piano. She also took a photo of Mom, David and Sue having "tea for three" at the small playroom table.

Mom had just baked bread so she invited Edith and Lois to have a sandwich made with fresh bread, "still hot," and served with strawberry preserves. They had never tasted anything so good and wanted to know the recipe for this delicious treat. She told the ladies, "I don't have a recipe. I just put in enough of this and enough of that and it always turns out."

Lois Hurley was so impressed that she said, "I want a picture of you putting together your ingredients for this bread." Mom finally agreed. She set up the proper bowls from the pantry next to her kitchen cupboard where there was a flour bin and enameled countertop and shelves for spices and most of her pans.

Edith and Lois thanked us over and over for all the information and pictures and then drove down the driveway. We thought this was the end of it, but when we received the July 15, 1944 issue of Wisconsin Agriculturist, there was the article about us, entitled, "Meet the Fortneys: All the Family Likes the Farm."

Mom said, "This is horrible! I didn't think they would put us in the magazine like this! I just had on my old everyday clothes and my hair was a mess. Your father didn't even get included."

Dad had been back by the woods cultivating corn and hadn't even known about the article until he came home for supper. He said, "I am proud of my kids and am glad to show them off to other people as an example of a happy family."

After several days Mom finally calmed down. This was not the end of the story, though. About a week after "Meet the Fortneys" came out in the magazine, our puppy got in the chicken house and started killing chickens. About eighty of them piled up in a corner and smothered. We sorted through the dead ones and then dug a hole and buried them. Dad took one dead chicken, tied it to the puppy's collar, and tied him up in the machine shed. He said, "By the time that rots off, he will be so sick of chickens that he will never look at one again." He was right.

We saved two pullets that had been injured and made a small fenced-in enclosure between the house and garden to use while they healed up again. We named them, guess what? Edith and Lois!

Edith must have been hurt worse than we knew. After about ten days, she died. Lois had a broken wing that healed but was not usable. It hung down and got in her way. We cut off the feathers, but that did not help. We saw right away that Lois needed special care. If she tipped over, she could not get back on her feet without help. Lois lived several years in the barn and ate feed with the cows. She hopped up the stairway to the haymow and laid her eggs on the landing near the top. With her bad wing, she had to jump up the stairs one step at a time. Fred and I made a nest for her to lay her eggs in, but she didn't like the nest and instead, would back up to the top step and lay her egg over the edge, with the egg breaking as it rolled down the steps.

One day Lois stopped laying eggs. Then she stopped eating, withered away and died. We kids had a funeral for Lois and buried her in our pet cemetery. Such is the story of farming as well as life. A full circle—birth, life, death, then birth again.

The Pheasant Project

One year for a 4-H project, Fred and I took Wildlife Management. Part of the project was to get pheasant eggs and hatch them out, raise the chicks and in the fall, release them into the wild. I got a couple of setting hens from Aunt Leone. Through the county office we got thirty fertile pheasant eggs and gave each setting hen fifteen eggs to incubate. They took to them just like they were their own. Fred and I were already "counting our pheasants before they hatched." We thought thirty eggs would equal thirty pheasants, but it just didn't happen that way.

First of all, some of the eggs didn't hatch. I believe we got twenty-one chicks. They were real wild and some died right away because their instinct told them to eat bugs and worms and buds off plants, not chicken feed from a man-made feeder. Now we were down to sixteen babies.

We were raising them in the old chicken house, which hadn't been used for anything for many years. We patched up all the holes we could find, but Susie's cats had been watching the pheasant babies through the windows every day and plotting and scheming to get in and eat our chicks. One day when we went up to feed the pheasants, we found a cat inside the chicken house eating baby pheasants. She had killed six of them and was so full she could hardly move. She got thrown out quite violently. Now we had ten chicks left. We inspected the entire chicken house and finally found a narrow slit in the wall where the cat must have squeezed through. There was no way she could have gotten out, with her belly full of pheasant.

All went well for a couple of weeks. We saw cats on the rooftop, though, peering through the upper windows, walking back and forth. We said to each other that we had them foiled now—they could never get in. Wrong. A couple of days later when we went to do the feeding, there a darn cat was, inside, eating a pheasant! How in the world did she get in? There could be only one answer. From the top of the roof to just above the floor was a ventilation tube made from four boards nailed together. That cat had discovered that this tube led to the chicks. I suppose she could smell them in the air coming from the tube. The inside of this tube was about four inches square and she would have had to shinny down the tube head first to get in.

We probably would have willingly "eliminated" some cats, but they were Susie's pets. Darned cat—by fall we had only five pheasants left to release into the wild. We took them down to the cow pasture and let them go, in a bushy area. This was the end of raising pheasants.

The Swine Project

Another 4-H endeavor was our swine project. Our farm always had hogs. In 1915 Ole T. built a two-story building for hogs, with the downstairs section for housing them, and outside, around two sides, a concrete floor with concrete feeders. The upstairs was a place for a feed mill and hog food, with a door to the west that connected to the corn crib. Really quite modern for 1915.

The building was remodeled about 1925 and the upstairs turned into a chicken house. We accepted as fact that every farm had both hogs and chickens. This was part of the philosophy that all farms should be diversified. Actually, diversification worked out well: dairy, tobacco, hogs and chickens. And, of course, fruit trees and a large vegetable garden. You never even considered that a farmer might purchase milk, butter, eggs, beef or pork, or any fruits or vegetables. These necessary items all came from the farm. Money for clothes and shoes came from the milk income. The tobacco check furnished money for new cars, college educations and trips. It's too bad life can't be this simple today, but times change.

When we enrolled in high school, both Fred and I took agriculture and joined FFA (Future Farmers of America). I was involved in dairy and crops. Fred had chickens and hogs. Part of the hog project was a program to raise purebred breeding stock. Fred got two bred gilts (young female pigs) and the plan called for caring for the gilts until they raised their little pigs. After this you would have to return two bred gilts to the FFA for someone else to do the same as you had done. The rest of the pigs were yours to do with as you pleased. Ideally you would breed these new young pigs and start your own herd. The males could be sold as breeding stock since they were all registered purebreds. This was a very good program, especially if you had facilities at home for hogs. Fred took hogs to the Vernon County Fair in Viroqua and also to the Wisconsin State Fair in Milwaukee, where he did quite well. Later he was picked for the County Judging Team for the State Fair.

These purebred pigs may have been well pedigreed, but they were still pigs. Pigs are born with an instinct to get out and these pigs must have thought about it every day. We thought we had a pig-proof fence, but they must have been smarter than us because it seemed like they got out all the time. Whenever they escaped they went straight to Mom's garden or the flowerbed around the house. Dad said maybe we needed to build an electric fence inside the other fence. That worked, but we still didn't trust them.

Living with Nature:
Birds, Animals, Bees

When you live on a farm you have opportunities to observe nature around you all the time. This was indelible memory-making that stayed with us our whole lives.

Birds are ever present. The majestic red-tailed hawk will make your heart beat faster when you see him soaring overhead. Once you get to know him, he is like a friend. One lived on our farm for many years. He had a perch on the power line north of our buildings. He always perched about two feet south of the third power pole from the top of the hill. From this vantage point he could see all the land on about one hundred twenty acres. If a mouse or rat ran across the field, invariably Hawk would catch him and have a snack.

Another delicacy was snakes. Our hired man saw Hawk pick up a large bull snake and fly away with it still writhing and trying to get away. Hawk knew what he was doing. He circled around, gaining altitude until he was at least three hundred feet high, then dropped the snake on a gravel road and followed it down. The poor snake was not only dead but tenderized. Hawk landed, picked up his prize and flew away again. This time the snake hung down from his talons like a wet rope!

When my wife, Jane, went to work, she always watched for Hawk. One fall day Hawk wasn't there and we never saw him again. He had either died of old age or someone shot him for target practice. Hawks are protected, but some people pay no attention to laws. Many years have passed, but we still miss Hawk.

We observed another hawk on a friend's farm near Readstown. We were helping with the haying and saw a red-tailed hawk dive out of the sky and kill a full-grown rabbit. He must have been a young hawk who could not gauge his strength because he tried to pick up the rabbit and fly away. Big problem! He couldn't get airborne. As we watched, he tried and tried, but could only get about two inches off the ground. Finally he gave up, dragged the bunny over to the shade of a tree and ate until he was full. This was a case of his eyes being bigger than his stomach.

Hawks can live to be ten or twelve years old, and some migrate to southern states in the fall.

There are two large birds that are mortal enemies: The common crow and the great horned owl. Owls are night birds and can see well in almost complete darkness. They are smart, too, and since they can fly silently in the dark, they locate the crows' roosting trees in advance. When they get hungry they just pluck a crow off his roost and he never knows what hit him. The crow is completely helpless.

But when the sun comes up in the morning, it is a different story. The crow flock will hunt out the owl's roost until they find him. Since owls are night birds they don't like to be out in daylight because their eyes cannot focus in bright sunlight. Now the crows have a heyday. There may be more than fifty birds in the flock. They fly at and torment the poor owl until he flies away and finds another tree. Owl thinks to himself, "Tonight I will kill two or three of those *@#% devil birds!" This has been going on for hundreds of years.

When brother Fred raised chickens there was one that grew faster and developed earlier than the rest. He named her Henny Penny. One night we forgot to chase the chickens out of the trees and lock them up. Next morning when we went down to the chicken yard to feed the pullets, Henny Penny was missing. We looked all over for her to no avail. That night when we went over in the pasture to chase the cows home, we found Henny Penny lying dead under the big oak tree. A great horned owl had killed her during the night and carried her to the tree to eat her. Why would that owl pick our Henny Penny out of the flock of three hundred chickens? He had pulled off most of her feathers and eaten about half her body. Under the blood on her behind we saw the end of an egg. This would have been her first egg. Fred cried and cried, but we gathered up what we could find, took her home, had a funeral and buried her in our pet cemetery. I am sure Henny Penny went to animal heaven. We had a very low opinion of owls after this disaster.

Crows are very smart birds. One summer morning I got up real early, took my .22 rifle and a crow call that I had bought uptown, and climbed up in a bushy tree. I could see a whole flock of crows over in Dad's cornfield. I blew on the crow call and the crows all grew silent. Then one crow left the group and flew straight toward me. He circled the tree, saw me, then went straight back to his crowd, calling caw-caw-caw all the way. They then all flew away with a caw! caw! caw!

The crow that flew over me was a sentinel and had flown back and warned his buddies to split.

In town there are crows living along the streets and they make their living by robbing dog food and cat food. They also seem to know who has thrown out table scraps in their trash cans. These smart crows will knock the lids off the cans and have a picnic. They seem to know if you just have paper trash in your can because they don't bother to stop. Town crows are all very fat.

Songbirds are part of your life when you grow up on a farm. They seemed to come back to our yard every year. Barn swallows appeared May 15 like clockwork. They built nests in the dairy barn and we could watch their families grow when we were helping with chores. The parents had a big job catching bugs and flies to feed the hungry babies. The bigger the babies got, the faster the parents had to go to keep up with their voracious appetites. When the babies were big enough to leave the nest, all our farm cats seemed to be sitting around the barn waiting to catch and eat the babies, but Mother Nature had prepared the babies for this problem. The very first time the babies left the nest, they could fly and land on a light wire outside the barn and be safe from the evil cats. We had cats that could jump three feet in the air to snag a low flyer, but they usually missed and we were glad because the birds were our friends.

There was an old dead tree, a maple, a short distance from our house when we were young that supported a wealth of wildlife. This was a den tree for woodpeckers and flickers, which are related to woodpeckers. They were not friends but did share the same tree, but not too close to each other. Squirrels lived in the hollowed-out center of the tree and sometimes at night when there was a full moon we saw owls sitting high in the old maple. Actually they were looking over the chicken yard and thinking about a chicken supper. These owls were not our friends.

Out in the fields we observed many birds that we do not see today. I remember meadowlarks, bobolinks, bluebirds and whip-poor-wills. Bluebirds lived in hollow wood fence posts. Wood posts are a thing of the past now, so if you want bluebirds you have to put up bluebird houses. This practice has limited success. Raccoons soon learn there are eggs or babies in these nests and help themselves to a treat. Of course robins are everywhere. The tiny hummingbird seems to be more numerous than when we grew up. I have never seen a hummingbird nest, but have heard that it is the size of a quarter and lined with spider webs. The two eggs are the size of peas.

We have some very large birds that we did not have years ago. The wild turkey is a common sight nowadays. We had a neighbor who said a wild turkey brought fifteen chicks up to her back door every morning to eat up the cat food. There is a hunting season for turkeys now and people come from many surrounding states to try their luck.

Another large bird we never saw years ago is the turkey buzzard. The buzzard is cousin to the bald eagle and lives on dead animals. Authorities say that a buzzard can smell dead flesh more than five miles away. It used to be that when deer became too numerous in our county, it was the county's expense to pick up deer killed by cars. This is no longer a problem as buzzards have taken over. Now dead animals are eaten up almost right away.

Bald eagles used to be seen only along major rivers, but we see them quite often around home now. I believe the eagle is now catching trout in our streams since the habitat has been improved and the trout population has mushroomed. They also eat deer killed by cars.

Some of the little animals we see are also interesting. The red fox is a beautiful masterpiece of nature. He lives on mice and bugs so he is a farmer's friend. Coyotes are quite common now. It makes the hair stand up on the back of your neck when they howl at night. Coyotes kill foxes because they think they are competing for their wild game. Their principal source of food is rabbits. They also kill and eat house cats!

One small creature that has all but disappeared is the wild honeybee. When we were young, Al Woolhiser, David's father, harvested a bee tree over in the woods. After locating the tree, he climbed up and plugged the hole where the bees went in and out. Al and our dad cut the tree down and then figured out the area in the tree that the honey was in. They cut in halfway with the saw, then took an ax and split out the piece of wood. There was the honeycomb—and the bees! Al had a smoker to confuse the bees. The hollow in the tree was clear full of honey! We took out pail after pail of honeycomb.

When we got back to the house our kitchen turned into a honey factory. Some we just ate out of the comb, but the rest we strained through a clean flour sack in back of the cook stove where it was warm. We got almost ten gallons of honey from that tree. Mother had to find a lot of recipes that called for honey. A good bee man like Al Woolhiser could identify the source of the honey by color and taste. There was wildflower honey, basswood honey, clover honey and fruit tree blossom honey. I think this honey lasted us several years.

Wild honey trees are now a thing of the past since disease has killed most of our wild bees. Tame bees are dying of the same diseases.

The Thompsons, our next-door neighbors, had a swarm of wild honeybees inside a wall of their old house. They contacted Holtan Jensen, who was a bee man, and asked him how to get rid of the bees. He came over and told them, "I will set up a hive in your yard and convince those bees not only to move in, but to move all their honey in, too." It took about three weeks, but that was the end of the bee problem. Mr. Jensen not only gained a swarm of bees, but a whole bunch of honey. He gave some to the Thompson family for the privilege of catching the colony of bees.

As we grew up, we learned to respect nature. Whether it was birds or animals around us, we felt they were all our friends and had an important place in our world. Dad did not hunt, but cousin David Woolhiser and I did. We felt hunting was a privilege and enjoyed every minute in the woods. To us, hunting was not all about killing animals, but about observing birds and animals that were around much of the time, but you did not see them because you did not know when to look. We felt we were harvesting some of the surplus species just as the Indians did many years ago. They thanked the souls of the animals for furnishing them with food. When we saw birds or animals that were rare, we lay still and watched them. There seemed to be a surplus of rabbits and squirrels, so these were the ones we shot and took home for Mother to cook. David Woolhiser's dad lived on the Mississippi River and hunted ducks and geese. Thousands of these birds migrated in the fall. Al Woolhiser was once a cook in a lumber camp, so was an excellent cook. He could cook up these wild ducks so they were especially delicious. We thought our rabbits and squirrels tasted real good, too, but I doubt if I could eat them now.

Home Grown Molasses
and Maple Syrup

When we were young, Dad said he thought we should grow some sugar cane so we could have our own molasses. We contacted a fellow by the name of Cap Stussey, who lived down along the Kickapoo River. Cap told us we should buy some "orange amber" seed. He said, "This is the best cane seed you can buy, but don't plant it in your best ground or the sap will be too watery. When you harvest it, take time and strip off all the leaves and also the seed head. If you don't clean up the stalks, you will get bitter syrup."

We followed his instructions to a T. When the cane was ripe in the fall, we stripped off the leaves and seed head and tied up the stalks in bundles.

Cap Stussey's syrup camp was a chapter from the past. The cane mill had rollers that squeezed the juice out of the stalks. The juice ran down a pipe to the evaporation pan. Cap Stussey burned wood for heat to evaporate the water out of the sap. The final product was a beautiful golden-brown molasses syrup that was just about perfect for pancakes and French toast or to put on bread for a sandwich.

When Cap Stussey died, so did his syrup business. Others tried to duplicate his system with a little modernization, but it just did not work. Now when we drive past the spot on the banks of the Kickapoo where Cap Stussey lived, we always feel a little pang of loss. We have never been able to buy molasses syrup that comes close to Cap Stussey's.

Another area specialty is maple syrup. What we have is 100% pure maple syrup made from the sap of our own trees. Sometimes in the store you see maple-flavored syrup, but when you read the fine print on the back of the bottle, it says 2% maple syrup and 98% corn syrup. This is an insult to our intelligence when we grew up on 100% maple syrup. People drive for many miles to buy a year's supply of the <u>real</u> stuff. Price is no object if you grew up on our local specialty.

The Amish community always buys farms that have plenty of maple trees. They harvest the sap from the trees and make maple syrup. Of course they always save enough for at least a year's supply for their own families, but they always seem to have a good supply to sell.

The syrup season starts early in the spring. When you have warm days and freezing nights you have the best sap runs. Sometimes the season can run for several weeks. If you have a late spring and it warms up fast and stays warm, the season can be over in just a few days. Most people have never tasted 100% pure maple syrup. If they are lucky enough to get it, they are sold on the taste and will drive a long way to get more of it. I think we take it for granted because we live in the center of southwest Wisconsin, where a lot of good things are produced.

Family Music

We have to thank our parents from the bottom of our hearts for all the care and concern they had for us while we were growing up. We kids may have been unruly and wild, but we were full of energy and ready to take on the world. Mom and Dad realized this and gave us every opportunity to develop any potential.

Dad told us he had always wanted to learn to play the piano, but his father, Ole T., told him, "Boys <u>farm</u>, period. End of discussion. Get to work!" Dad had had no choice, but he said, "If my children want to learn music, I will support them completely."

We kids started taking music lessons when I was ten years old. Fred was then eight-and-a-half and Sue was five. Our teacher was Mrs. Clayton Wheeler in Viroqua. She said Sue was too young and needed to learn to read first, so she could understand the music better. From the start Fred loved to play and would practice for hours. I hated to practice, but suffered through it for a year, until I played my final piece at a Christmas music recital, and the folks finally let me quit. Later on, the high school band teacher wanted me to learn how to play an instrument, but that didn't interest me any more than the piano had.

I'll back up to when we got our piano. We first discovered music when Fred and I each got a toy xylophone for Christmas and realized that the keys were the same as on the old organ in our parlor. Ole T. had purchased the old pump organ for his daughter Elisabeth. Nobody else played it. When we found out that we could make music on the organ, the next step was a piano. Mrs. Wheeler had a good used one, so Dad bought it for us.

In her store, Viesta Wheeler gave lessons and sold musical instruments and also music books and sheet music. Clayton Wheeler, her husband, was a good singer and often sang solos at the Methodist church in town. Her music store was sort of old fashioned and not well organized and I am sure that people stole sheet music and music books from her all the time. She ran the store all by herself and gave lessons in the store at the same time. Clayton Wheeler had a nervous problem and sometimes got very depressed and just sat at home by himself and looked out the window. There are now treatments for these problems and maybe he could have had a normal life and completely enjoyed himself.

I remember one Christmas Mrs. Wheeler had a piano recital at her home and all of her students performed (including me). It was a nice evening, with the piano next to the Christmas tree and a delicious Christmas lunch afterwards. Clayton Wheeler was having one of his "good days" and he made a very gracious host. They lived on the edge of town on Railroad Avenue.

Fred learned to play the piano very well and Sue became master of the keyboard and went on to play the organ as well. She went to Lawrence College at Appleton, Wisconsin, and earned a degree in music. She has given many concerts and is the director of music at a large church in La Crosse, Wisconsin. Sue's two daughters were both piano majors, too, and her son, Chad, played clarinet in the high school band.

Our brother David also learned to play the piano, but said, "So I can play the piano. So what?" However, he sang in the Viroqua Barbershop Chorus and married Julie Tracy from North Carolina. Julie has a doctoral degree in voice and teaches at a private school. My wife, Jane, is an excellent singer and she helped organize the local Sweet Adeline Chorus and was the director for several years. She also sang in a quartet called The Happi-Tones. Choir directing comes naturally to her and she has in the past directed several church choirs. Our daughter, Nicki, plays piano, clarinet and piccolo.

My dad's wish to have his family blossom in music came to pass, but sadly, it happened after he passed away. Freddy suffered a fatal heart attack at the age of sixty-four. He not only didn't hear the family music, but never saw any grandchildren. If we had had today's technology in 1960, a multiple heart bypass operation may have given him another twenty or twenty-five years of life. We have always felt and even yet feel his presence near as we watch our grandchildren mature and develop, especially when they take an interest in music and learn to sing or play an instrument.

Music soothes the soul and to those of us who grew up with it, I believe it is as necessary as oxygen to help us enjoy life.

Our parents, Alfred Lauritz Fortney and Ruby Jasperson Fortney

Exploring

When cousin David Woolhiser and I went exploring up and down the area valleys, we were always on the lookout for remains of old houses and even shacks and dugouts in hillsides. There had been old men living in some of them and our curiosity was always fired up to see if we could dig up things they may have left behind. Probably the most common item was empty whiskey bottles and broken dishes, including coffee cups.

We had heard tales about some of these people who lived in huts and shacks. One was about a fellow that lived in a shack that had a chicken wire ceiling covered with straw. One night he had company and they were drinking and talking. All at once they heard a rustling sound in the straw overhead and Little Oscar said, "Must be rats up there." He grabbed his shotgun and fired several shots into his ceiling. The rustling stopped, but then they heard drip, drip, drip on the floor. It was blood. There may have been rats up there or there could have been a coon or a possum or a tomcat. Whatever it was was now dead.

All of these derelicts had the same problem. They were illiterate and alcoholic. None was married and they worked around on farms just long enough to get money to buy more booze. When they worked for farmers they got meals and a paycheck on Friday night. Dad said, "Take this as a lesson. If you start drinking you will never amount to anything and you might end up just like these poor souls." This so inspired us kids that we decided we would never drink, ever!

One hot Saturday night my folks had gone to bed, but it was so hot they could not sleep. It was full moon and the sky was clear and cloudless. They were visiting as they lay there when all at once they heard singing outside. They went to the window and looked out. In the bright moonlight they could see two figures walking slowly down the road past the mailbox. It was two men and they were singing the hymn "Nearer My God To Thee" in two-part harmony. It was beautiful and very impressive. As they approached the ravine south of the farm the singing stopped abruptly. One man said in a terrified voice, "What was that?" The other said, "I heard it, too. There are lions and tigers down in that ditch. We must run for our lives!" Their hollering and screaming could be heard as they ran down the road and disappeared over the hill.

These guys were two of the local drunks who were walking home from town after a whole night of heavy drinking. Their imaginations had turned into hysteria. Some of these people lived out their lives in the area and neighbors pitied them and chipped in to pay for their funerals and gravestones after they passed away. Others moved away and were never heard from again. A few saved up their money and went back to Norway where they could be buried next to relatives. What sad and meaningless lives.

Oftentimes when we went exploring and had wandered down in Tainter Hollow, we would stop and go swimming in some of the deep pools in the stream. There were two problems. The streams had sharp rocky bottoms that cut and bruised our feet. Our parents didn't allow us to go barefoot. They said, "You will get hurt on all the sharp things that are unseen in the tall grass." Our feet never got tough like the feet of other kids who were allowed to go barefoot all summer. The other problem was the cold, cold water. Our streams in the steep narrow valleys were all fed by limestone springs all along the creek. Excellent temperature for trout, but shivering cold for boys to swim in. I was told that when the water comes out of the springs it is 49 degrees.

We would stretch out in the grass in the pasture along the creek and lie in the sun and daydream and talk about everything from frogs and fish to where does the water go when it leaves our valley. We didn't talk about girls yet. Girls were a pain in the neck and sometimes they spoiled our plans just to be ornery.

Was there a hole in the ground where the water went, just like a drain in a kitchen sink? Or did it flow into a pond or lake? David said he thought maybe it went into the Atlantic Ocean and mixed in with all the other water and maybe whales would someday swim in the same water that we had just swum in. David said, "When we get home, let's look it up in the encyclopedia and other maps that your folks have." I thought this sounded stupid, but after supper that night we asked Mother for some maps. We told her we needed a map of the valley, a map of Wisconsin, and one of the world, too. She said "How come you boys are so interested in geography all of a sudden?" We said, "Never mind, we have a reason."

We went in our bedroom with the maps and spread them out on our bed. Sure enough, Tainter Creek flowed into the Kickapoo River between Soldiers Grove and Gays Mills. The Kickapoo River joined the Wisconsin River at Wauzeka, the Wisconsin River emptied into the Mississippi just below Prairie du Chien, Wisconsin, and then after flowing a thousand miles south, the Mississippi spilled into the Gulf of Mexico at New Orleans, Louisiana. David was right after all! But I was sure that by then the creek water was so thinned out that you couldn't find it back. Oh well, water was water.

We planned for when I would go up to David's home at Stoddard, Wisconsin, again. Once a summer Fred and I would get a chance to go up to Stoddard to David Woolhiser's home for about a week. Stoddard is right on the Mississippi River and a railroad track goes right along the edge of town. This opened up a whole new set of adventures. We would go down to the river to fish or to explore. One of the things that really interested us was all the little creatures that lived in and next to the river. We hardly ever saw a turtle at home, but in the Mississippi backwaters there were hundreds of baby turtles about as big as a silver dollar. We always brought some home with us in a tin pail with river weeds and a little water to keep them moist and comfortable. We put them in our homemade ponds where we played farm at home and fed them angleworms, but for some reason they all died in about a week.

We couldn't believe how big and wide the Mississippi was compared to our little Tainter Creek. When we went barefoot in the sand and sat and dreamed, we could imagine old riverboats steaming up the river and log rafts floating downstream to some distant sawmill. We also imagined pirates coming and going and what if we had a raft? Could we just run away and live on the river like Huckleberry Finn? Could we go clear down to the southern states and see darkies working in the cotton fields or fishing for big catfish on the river? Maybe we had better just think and dream until next summer.

Stoddard was a kind of old fashioned river town. When we first visited up there they didn't have city water yet. Everybody either had a well or shared one with a neighbor. Then the men of the town got together and decided to dig in water mains themselves, without hiring a contractor. Most everybody had a shovel so they got together one day and started digging. They dug a ditch right down the middle of Main Street. In about three days the ditch was all dug. They planned to start laying the mains the next morning.

That night it rained real hard and after midnight the whole village shuddered for a few seconds. Nobody thought much about it until next morning. Alas, they had never thought about it when they were digging, but they had dug in pure sand. When the rain fell, the ditch collapsed and all the sand fell in. It all had to be dug out again. This time they drove in posts and nailed up planks to hold back the sand. This was just the start of the project. They had to dig in pipes to all the houses, too. If anybody didn't want to help pay for pipes or help dig, they didn't get water.

Next was to dig a pipe over to the bluff and up to the new reservoir. There were no engineers in the crew. The guys decided to go three-fourths of the way to the top of the hill so they could get plenty of pressure. They worked all summer and finally got done. When the water was turned on, the water pressure was so high that if you opened a faucet halfway, the water would hit the sink and come right out and up and hit you in the face. If you wanted to get a glass of water and didn't hold on real tight, the water would knock the glass out of your hand and you would get broken glass in your face. The women were afraid to even turn the water on.

Someone said, "Maybe we should go up to La Crosse and talk to some professional plumber and see what we can do about this problem." They got a guy to come down to Stoddard and look around. He asked, "Where is your water supply?" He was told, "You can see it way up on the hill over there." He exclaimed, "You stupid fools! With that much fall you probably have over 250 pounds pressure. You will have to plumb in a pressure regulator. We don't have any that go that high so I'll have to get one out of Chicago, Illinois. You are lucky you didn't blow up the whole system. It will take a while to get the right equipment to do the job."

Now the talk around town was about the super water pressure. A fire department had been organized, but there had not been any fires. Someone said, "I bet we could really put out a fire now." A couple of the boys in town heard this and thought, "If we don't have a fire before that stupid regulator gets here, we will never know." There was an old barn on the edge of town and they went back there one day after dinner with some matches and kerosene and lit it, then ran back uptown yelling, "Fire! Fire!" Everybody in town came out to see all the fun. The fire department got there in about two minutes and hooked up the hoses. Two of the biggest men in town held the hose and when the water came out, it knocked the barn flat, after peeling off the roof first. Some of the burning boards were thrown fifty feet in the air. The barn was gone but only part of the boards were burned.

Most of the old timers around town were practical jokers, too. Just down the street from Woolhiser's gas station was another gas station. There were always five or six guys sitting around telling jokes, fish stories and tall tales. This station didn't have plumbing, but had outdoor toilets. The owner was the biggest joker of all. He said, "Look out the window at the ladies' can. See that fat woman going in? I put a loudspeaker down in the hole. Just wait until she gets set down." He picked up a microphone and said "Lady, could you use the other hole? I'm working down here." She let out a scream, the door burst open and she ran down the street, still pulling up her panties. The old codgers laughed until they were practically rolling on the floor.

One year when we went up to Stoddard Aunt Blanche took us up to the La Crosse circus, Barnum and Bailey's. We went to La Crosse from Stoddard on the bus that went up and down the river. At the bus terminal on Fourth Street we took a city bus to the fairgrounds. Fred and I had never ridden a bus before so this alone was a big thrill. A three-ring circus with lions, tigers and elephants was beyond our wildest dreams. There were cowboys and Indians and trapeze artists, too. The circus had come to town on the train and had a parade down the street to the fairgrounds. It seemed like everybody and his brother was there. I had never seen so many people in one place before. There were side shows with freaks and exotic dancers. We wanted to go to see the dancers, but Aunt Blanche said, "Absolutely not! Those women are barely dressed and a sinful show like that should be banned." We didn't understand why. She said, "The big city has many sinful things that children shouldn't see. You kids are better off at home where we can watch you."

We were shocked when the big boys at Stoddard used swear words all the time, including words we had never heard before. Aunt Blanche didn't know this, though. Uncle Al swore all the time, but he was a grownup and some of them did this. Fred and I could almost feel our ears burning and we thought that these people who swore all the time would all go to hell someday. We were glad to get back home again on Saturday to our pets and parents. The next day we all went to church together.

The Big Oak Tree

The oak tree in our yard, as mentioned in the "Climbing Trees" chapter, was one of our fondest memories. Dad had put a rope up on the long limb on its north side so we kids could have a swing. We would swing for hours and let our imaginations run wild. We imagined Indians resting under our tree a hundred years before the white man came to southwest Wisconsin. Maybe they were braves or maybe they were children just playing Indian games, who knew? Maybe a hunter chased a bear up our tree and shot it and later made a bearskin robe to keep his children warm on a cold winter night. If trees could talk, maybe they would tell secrets about their past. Our tree was a rare species of oak that is almost extinct. Alan Jones, a well educated forester who lived here years ago, could not identify it.

The big oak tree in winter 1940, crown width 65 feet.
Barely visible are electric wires, first installed in 1939
by the Rural Electrification Administration

The oak was located near the old house, the one that was replaced by the big house we now live in. Its spreading branches made shade for the old house. Different events happened under the old oak tree. Late one night when my dad was young there came a knock on the door, after eleven o'clock. There stood a young couple who said they wanted to get married. They had a marriage license with them and Ole T., my grandfather, who was a justice of the peace, said, "Sure, I can do it. I'll wake up two of my boys to be witnesses and we'll take care of you."

They lit a couple of lanterns and put them under the old oak tree. Grandfather "tied the knot" and the newlyweds went happily on their way. He probably married other people, too, but this was the only couple we ever heard about.

One time late at night the family was awakened by a voice under the oak tree calling, "Father! Father! Father!" Ole T. was a light sleeper and jumped up to see what the fuss was about.

Thinking someone was in deep trouble, he answered, "What is the problem? How can I help you?"

The voice spoke up, "Father, I need two dollars to fix my wagon."

Ole T. said, "I am a blacksmith and I can fix your wagon for you."

The voice replied, "No, I need two dollars to fix my wagon."

Ole T. was suspicious now. He looked down the driveway and in the moonlight, he saw two gypsy wagons down by the road. He knew this gypsy was just trying to work him for some money and decided to have a little fun with him, so he replied, "Just bring your wagon up and I will fix it for you."

The voice replied, "No, I need two dollars to fix my wagon."

This argument went on and on for about fifteen minutes and finally the gypsy man stomped down the driveway grumbling to himself, "Dumb stupid Norwegian, dumb stupid Norwegian, dumb stupid Norwegian." They never saw the gypsy again.

In the summer of 1960 during a windstorm the big oak tree blew down. This was like losing a family member. Dad had died the same year in April and Mother was reminded of Dad's passing and said, "It seems like tragedy comes in pairs, first Dad and now our old oak tree."

The tree was hollow. Only a thin shell of sound wood had kept it standing. We cut it up for wood to burn in the house for heat. We blocked off the trunk starting at the bottom. When we got to about 16 feet, the tree was sound clear to the center. At this level we counted 224 growth rings and if you allowed 35 years for the tree to grow so the main trunk was this size, the tree would have been 259 years old when it blew down. Our big oak tree grew out of an acorn in 1701! This would have been 147 years before the first of our family arrived from Norway. This makes us seem awfully insignificant, doesn't it?

As the years went by, the ground kept sinking where the old oak tree stood. This was because the roots were rotting down.

There must have been a lot of large roots because we have refilled the hole probably four times.

We have Norway spruce planted on the sides of our lawn. I helped plant them when I was only six years old. They now tower more than 60 feet tall and have become almost family members. One Norway spruce replaced the blue spruce mentioned in the "Dogs" chapter in the beginning of this book. As long as I am alive I will make sure that nobody cuts any of them down.

There was a large hard maple south of the house that had been here since before the white man settled this land. I remember my dad telling about one time when he was young that some strangers came to visit. They were descendants of people that had first lived on this farm. An old blind lady who was with them said, "Take me out to my old maple tree." They did and she was so pleased. She said, with tears in her eyes, "When I was a little girl, I played around my maple tree and I could just reach my arms clear around the trunk. Maple was my best friend."

The maple tree blew down in a storm two years ago. The center was so rotten that we could not count the growth rings. The stump is still there and we will use it for a flower bed until it completely rots away. There is a replacement maple tree growing a short distance from the tree but it will take several lifetimes for it to get to the size of old maple.

Maybe it is silly to get nostalgic about a tree, but trees are living things in our world and when you realize how short a human life span is, and that some of our majestic trees could easily live up to three times as long as a man, we truly must give them respect. Most of our country was at one time covered with forests. The early settlers cut down most of these trees and sold the logs to timber buyers. Soon the land was barren. It has taken more than 150 years to change the mindset of man and "let nature get back to nature." The philosophy now is that if you cut down a tree, you must plant two trees for replacement.

There are also "weed trees." Some of these would be willows, ash and box elder, locally known as "piss elm." These trees are no good for lumber, make poor fire wood and if you don't keep after them, they creep into a field and eventually completely take over. Another tree that is a fast grower and has bad habits is the black walnut. The lumber is highly prized and very valuable, but walnut produces autotoxicity in the soil and will kill any tree that tries to grow near it. Walnuts want all or none. This is why we have respect for our oaks, maples and hardy pine, to name a few.

We watch the walnuts and as soon as they are big enough to sell we cut them down and turn them into cash. Burning walnut wood in a fireplace can be a bad practice because under the right conditions, the smoke can be toxic and you can get very sick. Walnut can get revenge on you for killing it even after it is dead.

Alida Ruby

On the night of January 6, 1898, during a blizzard, a tiny baby girl was born on Belgium Ridge Road in rural Vernon County to Sophia and Andrew Jasperson. Their fourth child, she was quite frail and weak and in a few weeks, came down with pneumonia. The doctor in Viroqua was summoned, and he didn't give much hope for this tiny baby. He told the parents they should call the minister to come out and baptize little Alida Ruby, because she would never live until spring.

But Sophia said, "By the grace of God, I am confident that the baby will survive and live a long and productive life."

Ruby Fortney and her firstborn, Tommy

Against all odds she did live, and four more children were born after Alida Ruby. Then, at age forty-six, Andrew Jasperson died of tuberculosis, on October 19, 1909. On the day of the funeral neighbors came to the farm to help dress the children and load them up in the wagon for the trip to the church. One neighbor said, in a somber tone, "Mark my words, in one year all these children will be dead, too." He said this where the little children could all hear him. His belief was that they probably all had TB and could not survive. Just think how crushed these kids must have felt to hear this, right after their father had died.

After the funeral the family stayed with friends in town for several days so the house could be fumigated. I don't know that this process did any good. People didn't know much about disease control and thought that after a person died of a disease, the house was still full of germs and that fumigating would kill all the bugs.

Sophia was now left with a farm and seven young children, five girls and two boys. Another son, Adolph, had died as a small child. Sophia decided to rent out the farm and live in town until Wallace was twelve years old. Then, by using light harnesses for the horses, and with the help of his sisters, Wallace could run the farm. This was almost unheard of back then. Women didn't have a place in farm ownership or farming. Sophia came from an era when the man was the supreme boss and the woman was expected only to have babies and feed and clothe them. In other words, she was almost a slave! Sophia decided she would break that mold and see that her daughters got an education and could make a difference for mankind.

My mother, Alida Ruby, went one year to high school and then transferred to teachers college. When she was seventeen years old she took a teaching job in a country school near home. Later she went out to Minnesota to teach. After several years of teaching she decided that nursing was her calling and went to school in Peoria, Illinois. Her sister Esther went with her.

When they graduated they stayed on in that hospital for several years.

Then Ruby, Esther, and two classmates, sisters named Ruth and Regina Wedapole, decided to go to California and work in a hospital in Santa Barbara. They loaded up their car with all their belongings plus three extra spare tires, an ax, a shovel, and some other tools. For 1928 this was an awesome adventure for four women. Some of the roads were barely passable. One day in a sandstorm they kept getting stuck and having to cut sagebrush to put under the wheels to get out. Along came a cowboy on horseback. He looked at them and shook his head. "Your biggest problem, ladies, is that you are two hundred yards off the highway and stuck in the desert. I've heard of women drivers, but this takes the cake!"

Their adventures were many. On days off they saw the national parks, went out to Catalina Island, visited the home of Zane Grey, went to many parties and met many interesting people. One night they met a young man who was selling real estate. He told them, "I can get you a bargain basement price on property in a new development near here. It will only go up in value and you can sell it and make a big profit." They said, "We'll take it. Let's close the deal." Now they owned part of California.

All well and fine, but nobody tried to buy their property. Every year they got a real estate tax statement, which they always paid. They had been taken, but no one would admit it. Finally, years after the four women had returned to Wisconsin, somebody somehow went out west and checked the land description. It was in the bottom of a bay under six feet of water. Sometime in the 1960s they received a letter explaining that this bay was going to be filled and a developer wanted to buy their property. They sold it immediately and that was that.

After a year in the west, the four of them came home. Ruby's younger sister Leone was then teaching at the Hinkst School. At the school picnic at the end of the school year, Alfred "Freddy"

Fortney noticed a cute young lady who had come with her sister to the picnic. They went for a walk in the woods that day and fell head over heels for each other. In June 1930 they were married. Ruby at that time was five feet and one-half inch tall and weighed 99 pounds. She was thirty-two years old and Freddy was almost thirty-six. Ruby hated the name "Alida" and never went by it, so she was Ruby to everyone that knew her. She signed her married name as Ruby Jasperson Fortney.

Almost overnight Ruby made the change from career girl to married life with its responsibilities and joys and heartaches. She and Freddy shared the big house with his parents, Ole T. and Karn Fortney. A diabetic, Ole T. was one of the first people in Wisconsin to take insulin. Naturally Ruby the nurse stepped right in to care for Ole T., who had other problems and eventually became an invalid and spent the last year of his life upstairs in his bedroom. He passed away on December 27, 1935. Karn suffered from arthritis, had a hard time getting around and had a heart spell that was taken care of back then by extended bed rest. She fell and cracked a hip and spent one winter in a bed in the dining room. She passed away in the spring of 1939.

I was the first child born to Ruby and Fred, in 1932. David was the fourth, born in 1939. Ruby really had her hands full with four children born in six-and-a-half years, and doctoring and caring for the old folks at the same time. We had hired girls during those years, but I think sometimes they were more bother than they were worth.

Ruby was the Sunday School Superintendent at church starting when Fred and I were big enough to attend. She felt she had an obligation to hold it all together and continued for twenty-five years, until 1965. She was active in Ladies Aid at church, organized the Silver Lining Club, volunteered for the Red Cross, was a 4-H leader at Belgium Builders Club, doctored everybody's aches and pains, and had enough grit to stand toe to toe with the Devil and spit in his eye!

Dad passed away April 8, 1960 from a heart attack. This was so sad because he and Mom were just starting to enjoy retirement. He was just sixty-four years old and had not even received his first Social Security check. They had been married twenty-nine years. Ruby was a widow for fifteen years, just a little over half as long as my parents were married. She kept busy with all her projects and enjoyed her first grandchildren.

I will always remember her and dad talking "big folks talk" when we were young children, and we would ask, "What did that mean?" An example: The folks went to a house party one night and discussed it the next day. Mom in referring to one neighbor said to Dad, "He makes my flesh crawl. I can feel him looking right through my clothes!" We asked her what she meant and she replied, "Someday you will know." This was a standard answer that always left us wondering. "He is a boozer . . . Someday you will know." "The Devil has him by the big toe . . . Someday you will know." "She was under the power of the Devil . . . Someday you will know."

Ruby passed away more than thirty years ago, but we still feel her presence as we watch our grandchildren grow up. She died in 1975 at the age of seventy-seven.

While an inpatient at Vernon Memorial Hospital, she slipped into a coma. We were all in her room when she woke up again. Her testimony touched us all and we will never forget it. She said, "While I was gone, I experienced an introduction to heaven. A feeling of no pain and an exquisite feeling of peace and well being. There was beautiful music playing and singing of angels all the time, with inspirational hymns I had never heard before."

She came home and stayed with us for a week. Her memory had slipped a bit and she needed help writing letters. It was like she had been given a short time to say farewell and to give some last minute instructions. She told us, "Do not let them hook me up to tubes and monitors. The Lord will take me when He is ready."

My sister, Sue, was pregnant at that time with her first child. Ruby told us "You will have to tell Sue's little girl about me." I don't know how Ruby knew it was going to be a girl, but she was very positive. Maybe the Lord told her while she was in the coma.

Blessed be the memory of Ruby.

Our mother, Alida Ruby Jasperson Fortney

Tobacco, the Devil's Crop

In 1870, only one acre of tobacco was raised in Vernon County, Wisconsin. By 1930 almost 9,650 acres were raised here. Most people in our country do not realize that tobacco will grow this far north. They believe it will grow only in Kentucky and other southern states. I have news for them. Tobacco has been grown in Wisconsin for more than 130 years.

Tom Fortney in tobacco field by barn

Two areas of Wisconsin are famous for tobacco: Vernon County, known as the northern area, and Dane County, known as the southern area. Both counties lie 100% in the Driftless Area, which 70,000 years ago was missed by the great glaciers that at one time covered most of North America. (See the "Driftless Area" chapter for more detail.) We have a weather pattern that is quite predictable, conducive to tobacco growing, and the soil is very rich, which is required for a good crop. The plants are started in a hot-bed and transplanted in the field in early June. In about 70 days it is ready to harvest. The cured dry leaves yield up to 3,000 pounds to the acre. At today's prices this would amount to up to $5,250 per acre. No other crop (except marijuana) comes close to this.

Riding the planter to get tobacco seedlings into the ground

Tom and son James viewing a good tobacco crop

Workers harvesting tobacco

Tobacco curing in the shed

Old-timers say that you cannot claim to know how to raise tobacco until you have raised at least five crops. Tobacco leaves are 12 to 18 inches wide and up to 30 inches long. Five minutes of hail will make your crop totally worthless. An early frost can be just as destructive. If the temperature drops below 31 degrees for more than 15 minutes, the crop is completely ruined and all your work is for naught. Some old-timers said, "Tobacco is the Devil's crop and if you are not willing to gamble with the worst of them, you have no business raising this crop."

Farmers are to a certain extent gamblers and when we were growing up my dad always raised tobacco. I first helped plant when I was ten years old. We had a one-row transplanter pulled by horses. The hired man and I rode the planter and put the plants into the ground. Dad drove the horses. You had to go extremely slow or the planters couldn't keep up and plants would get missed. We had about seven acres of tobacco and it took eight or ten days to plant. Next came cultivating and hoeing.

When harvest time came everybody pitched in. Dad said, "Hurry home from school so you can help pile tobacco!" We kids pitched right in and thought we were really helping. A grownup could pile more than ten times as much tobacco as little kids. We didn't realize it at the time, but we were learning the work ethic and responsibility.

The tobacco plants were speared on a lath about four feet long (five plants to each lath), then hung up in the tobacco shed to cure. In December if we got a foggy day to soften up the brittle leaves, we could take them from the hanging poles in the tobacco shed and strip off the leaves and pack them into a bale. Usually the tobacco buyers would come around in January and buy the crop. We never trusted them, though, because they took advantage of anyone they didn't like.

A former neighbor learned this the hard way. Tobacco was selling for eighty cents a pound. When a buyer came to Martin's farm and offered him eighty cents, Martin said, "The first one of you crooked thieves that offers me a dollar a pound can have my crop." The buyer was noticeably insulted and said, "We will see about that."

No more buyers came around after that. Martin was getting desperate. He went to all the tobacco companies in town and begged them to come out and bid on his tobacco. They said they would, but no one came. Evidently after he insulted the first buyer, the word got around and all the other buyers got together and said, "Let's teach that smart ass a lesson." Along about the first week in April, lo and behold, here comes a tobacco buyer to see Martin.

Martin said, "Are you ready to pay one dollar a pound?"

"No," said the buyer. "My top price to you is twenty-five cents a pound. You can't eat it, you can't sleep with it, if you try to keep it until next year it will spoil. You have no other choice." The buyer started to get back in his car.

Martin said, "Wait, wait, can't you do better than that?"

"No," said the buyer. "I could have offered you ten cents a pound. I feel I'm being real generous with you. You have thirty seconds to decide or I will drive away and you will be left holding the bag."

Martin accepted the twenty-five-cent offer. That was the last year he ever raised tobacco.

Tobacco over the years has paid for farms, barns and new houses. Paid for the first car or pickup truck for young men. Paid for college educations for many young people. Helped pay for new churches and hospitals, even if preachers didn't want to admit it.

Our area tobacco is not used in cigarettes but in high quality cigars and chewing tobacco.

Tobacco has been so demonized by the medical profession and the media that fewer than one hundred acres are still raised in this area. In our lifetime we have seen an industry grow and mature and also slowly die. We have seen a major source of area income dry up, with nothing to replace it.

When tobacco first appeared in Vernon County, the early Norwegian settlers got interested. Here was a crop that did not require a big investment and you could get enough income out of ten acres to pay for a farm in one year. In Norway if you did not inherit a farm and had to buy one, you had to get a 100-year loan and the approval of all your neighbors and even the church. If you had to go this route, it would take three generations to pay for a farm. This tobacco crop in America seemed like a dream come true.

Most farms for sale had very poor houses on them and the plan would be first to pay off the farm and then build new outbuildings, again paid for by tobacco. The last project would be a new house. This could all be accomplished in about six years. Some farmers went to town and became businessmen. The Bekkadal brothers in Westby were farmers who became tobacco buyers and also speculated in real estate. They said that they were broke twice and millionaires twice. Anybody that worked with tobacco knew about them.

We all heard stories where farmers got cheated out of their crops by crooked tobacco buyers. Then about twenty years ago we thought they were finally on the up and up, but the same thing happened again. We thought all the crooked buyers had died and gone to hell, but some must have come back in the dark of night and infected their offspring. When buying began, buyers went around and bought selected crops just from their buddies and friends and ignored everyone else. We had to put our crops through government grading and take a much lower price. The local co-op built a bunch of new warehouses to store this tobacco. How did they know in advance that these warehouses were needed? After everybody got their tobacco delivered to the warehouses the buyers came and bought up the crop from the government, for probably one-half of what it was worth, and made out like bandits. A lot of farmers quit raising tobacco and milked more cows instead. After getting jerked around for just so long you get tired of it and say enough is enough!

It was getting almost impossible to get help for harvesting, too. About the only people available locally were old men seventy-five to eighty years old, drunks and jailbirds. Even the jailbirds didn't want to work if it was hot weather or if it interfered with their favorite shows on TV at the jail. You could get them released for a day at a time under the Huber Act. You were then responsible for them for the day.

Maybe we are better off without the Devil's crop, but it was fun to see this crop grow. In the final stages of growth, it would almost double in size in the last fifteen days before harvest.

Our first tobacco crop, two plants in Mom's garden

Family Reunions

In past generations when families got together, they went all out. Grandma Karn enjoyed lots of company. She would start preparations many days in advance. It was normal for her to bake ten or twelve pies for a reunion dinner and have the men kill ten or twelve chickens. Peeling potatoes must have been a project, when you peeled fifty to seventy-five pounds at a time, especially when you were baking bread at the same time—ten to twelve loaves. Grandma always had lots of sauces on hand down in the basement. A favorite was peach sauce. This was stored in one-quart and two-quart glass jars. She would probably bring up five or six two-quart jars to make sure there would be enough to go around. On top of all this food, everybody that came would bring cakes and more pies, hot dishes and salads. Nobody had an excuse to go hungry.

Grandfather Ole T. Fortney sitting in his new 1924 Buick.
Uncle Malvin did the driving.

Tables were set up on the front porch as well as out on the lawn and inside the house. The local families that came to the reunion would be Arthur and Ida Fortney and their children; Ernie and Ada Tollefson and their family; Sam and Chistena Solverson (Chistena was a sister to Ole T.) and their nine children—and their children's children; Aunt Mary's family, Elvin and Florence and their five children; the Monson gang including Melvin and Tolia Monson and their three boys, Gayhart and Eloise Monson and their two girls, and Thomas and Adelaide Monson, who had no children. The Borgen and Wintz families were also included. Now we had well over one hundred people for dinner. Those fifteen chickens would not have gone very far, but the food everybody else brought made up the difference.

If all the Fortney clan from Dunn County came, you could almost double the number of people. It seemed like everybody that had a reunion tried to outdo the others. That was OK, though. There was always a fierce competition between those that farmed to top the clan as to the newest and most expensive automobile or tractor, or the biggest corn or tobacco, or the most or the best cows.

Selmer Solverson and his son, Alan, always said they would like to have a reunion of immense proportions and the day before, rent or borrow a new tractor, the biggest and most expensive available, and park it on the lawn for the weekend. They would not tell anybody about it, but would just listen to comments and watch the others turn green with envy, and just laugh to themselves. How many, they wondered, would hurry to the dealer on Monday morning and order a bigger tractor?

The present generation is much more scattered around the country and harder to gather together. The Dunn County branch of the Fortney clan still has reunions about every five years. People come from many states, but it is necessary to have name tags because you do not recognize the faces of some of your own relatives.

The Dunn County branch of the family tree originated with Hans T. Fortney, a brother to my grandfather, Ole T. Fortney. Hans and Mary moved to Dunn County in 1907. They had nine children at that time and moved mostly by train—cattle, horses, machinery and family. Most of the children had measles at the time, so it must have been a miserable trip. Six years after this big move a tenth child was born, a girl that they named Myrtle. Hans and Mary were both over fifty years of age by then. Was Myrtle a love child?

At one of the first reunions that I can remember, we kids were playing in the big sandbox down under the big oak tree in our yard. For some odd reason the sandbox always smelled like cat poop. We didn't know why. We thought wet sand always had that smell.

One of the Monson boys sent me to the house to get some water to wet down the sand. The kitchen was full of women all talking at the same time. It was almost a dull roar. I squirmed in through the crowd and all I could see was legs and high heels. When I finally got to the sink, I just could not get anybody to understand me and when I started to cry, some woman I had never seen before said, "What you need is a nap." She scooped me up and carried me to the sewing room and plopped me down on the bed and I cried myself to sleep. When I woke up the party was over and everybody had gone home. Here I had missed dinner and lunch and most of a day of playing! Mother and Grandmother had never missed me. I felt so bad. The next day they apologized all over the place, but I never forgot that day.

Reunions sometimes brought relatives from as far away as California, North Dakota, Michigan and Missouri. I don't know how they kept track of all these people. When I was little I hadn't ever seen some of these folks before. We played with the kids at the reunions, but when we saw them years later they had grown up and changed. Thanks to name tags you could probably figure out who some of them were.

It is interesting to note that this big extended Fortney family—fifteen hundred at last count—which started out in this country more than one hundred fifty years ago, all as farmers, has branched out all over the United States into so many different occupations. Many are in the teaching profession, some are lawyers and doctors, there are airline pilots, nurses, librarians, famous musicians, and others in occupations too numerous to mention. Some still farm, but farmers are now few and far between.

When my mother was still living she did a great job keeping track of everybody. Her Christmas card list had almost three hundred names on it. We are even now finding little notes she filed away and photo negatives she put between pages in old books. These open up different connections to people we barely knew.

The Roaring 40

Less than one mile downstream from Hinkst School, just before you come to the Slack Hill that takes you up to the ridge again, you come to what was known as The Roaring 40. An insurance man named Bud Slack, from Viroqua, bought this land in the late 1930s. He had a dream of building a country cottage hideaway, a place to relax. He also dreamed of an apple orchard on the hill that would make him rich.

Bud Slack built a rustic cottage, mostly from native timber. He built the cottage right around a tree, which then came out of the floor and extended through the ceiling. Quite spectacular for a stern community like ours. There was a large fireplace in the living room and a kitchen where they could prepare large meals. The room where the tree grew up through the floor was also used as a dining hall. Many people could be seated for banquets. Outside was a spring-fed pond with planted trout, a wishing well with water in the bottom and a wooden bucket attached to a windlass to pull up buckets of water. On the hill behind the cottage was a rustic path with stone steps. You could go up these steps, then up the path into the woods. There you could find many varieties of wildflowers and see native birds and squirrels as well as white squirrels that Slack had live-trapped in town and then turned loose on his property.

Neighbors called the apple orchard "a rich man's folly." Slack did not talk to anyone or seek any advice concerning growing apples. He decided to have just one variety of apple, which the Gays Mills orchards did not grow, and get a corner on the market for his specialty.

He first logged off the hillside, then removed the brush and stumps. The apples he planted were Dolgo crab apples, a very small apple that is used for pickles. They are smaller than one-and-a-half inches in diameter. When the trees started bearing, Slack went to Gays Mills and approached the big orchards about leasing his orchards and harvesting the fruit.

He was told, "Are you mad? You can't find anyone to pick those little bullets. We pay people by the bushel to pick and you would be hard pressed to pick two bushels a day of those tiny apples, and even if you could hire people to pick by the hour, you could not find enough people to pick off of your 125 trees when they are just at peak quality for pickling. We do not want to get involved with you at all!"

Slack was able to hire some local people to pick and they picked one truckload of apples. A trucker then took them to Milwaukee and spent most of a week trying to find a buyer. He finally found one who said, "I will give you $125 for the load. Take it or leave it."

When the trucker returned with the bad news, Slack lost interest in the whole mess and abandoned the orchards for good. The only use made of the orchards was that he let neighbors pick a few for pickles and jelly. The wild deer didn't mind. They loved crab apples and feasted every year when the apples fell off the trees.

Slack hired an old couple as caretakers of the property. They lived in an old house across the creek. They kept the grass all mowed and had two horses and two cows and raised tobacco in the fields. There was a log barn where they kept their horses and cows. Very picturesque! If neighborhood boys tried to go fishing on the property, Mr. Jensen would come with his shotgun and chase us off. I doubt he would have shot at us, but we were not about to stick around and find out. Mr. Jensen had a nephew who played with a group called the "Norske Spellemen." They sometimes played for us at the Hinkst Community Club.

Mr. Slack was quite community minded. He would open up his cottage to churches for a place to have picnics. Sometimes celebrities stayed there as a place to relax and get away from it all. Freddie Slack, a band leader from California, was a guest for a time, as well as others we did not know. Political parties had rallies and picnics at the cottage.

One happening was quite controversial in our stern Norwegian community—contractor parties that took place annually for some years at Slack's cottage. Local people were not allowed. Slack would invite contractors from all over the state to come to his summer bash. The only thing that could be a reason for these parties was to convince these guests to buy insurance from Slack, Nelson and Kassel.

Strange cars and trucks would go up and down our roads for several days before the party. A stage would be built and set up with special lighting. Bars would be built just for the night. People would start arriving shortly after noon. By twilight the party would be getting into full swing. Liquor flowed like water and the dancing girls kicked up a storm. We lived two miles away, but could hear the bands playing all night. The whole valley was covered with cars. Some were even from out of state.

The next morning, all was quiet in the valley and cars were seen leaving up until noon. Slack, who was quite influential in Viroqua, evidently had warned the police department to "stay away and don't mess with our party or our guests."

The mothers of Hinkst Hollow considered these parties as a den of sin and under the control of the power of the Devil. They predicted that Bud Slack would pay dearly when he met Saint Peter at the Pearly Gates. The men of the community stayed silent. I think they secretly wished they could have gone to the party, if they could have gone without Ma finding out.

The Driftless Area

Billions of years ago when the earth was young, our planet was pounded by dust storms and hundreds of years of strange weather. Great glaciers formed in the north as they extended south and at one time or another covered a good share of North America. The most recent glacier came south about 70,000 years ago. For some reason, the glacier parted and went around an area in southwest and west central Wisconsin. Earlier glaciations also parted and went around somewhat the same area.

We live in the center of this unique area. The last glacier melted about 8,000 years ago. We are continually amazed by what we learn about the area where we have lived our whole lives. Vernon County, Wisconsin, is an area of steep narrow valleys and flat prairie land. Before the valleys were formed by erosion, according to geologists, this area was the bottom of a shallow sea. We have many stone quarries and if you study the layers of limestone you can find fossils of water creatures and in some places, layers of oyster shells. The theory is that billions of years ago the surface of the earth changed and the upper midwest was thrust upwards and high above the water level of this prehistoric sea. This was before the era of the great glaciers.

When you study the geology of our world and discover the timeline of when different things happened you find that man has been here for only a nanosecond in comparison and one lifetime is less than a heartbeat.

The Kickapoo River, which runs entirely in the Driftless Area, is one of the oldest rivers in the world. Geologists tell us it is possibly 600 million years old. We live less than ten miles from it. The Kickapoo River is a subject for another day. People have been fighting Ma Kickapoo for more than 160 years, but Ma Kickapoo always wins.

In the Driftless Area, you will find 99.9% of the caves in the upper midwest. Any other caves were either erased or covered over by the great glaciers.

The Driftless Area is really quite small. From north to south it measures about 150 miles and is less than 100 miles at its widest. Most of it lies in Wisconsin, but it also includes a narrow strip of Minnesota and Iowa in the west and a small part of Illinois to the south.

There is a theory that early man traveled across the ice fields and discovered this land, which was an oasis in the world of ice and inhabited by animals that were trapped by the surrounding ice fields. In 1897 the skeleton of a prehistoric hairy mastodon was discovered a short distance from here near Boaz, Wisconsin. This skeleton is now on display at the University of Wisconsin-Madison. The mastodon has been extinct for almost a million years. Was he trapped here by the ice fields? Who knows?

We have a unique combination of natural soil, fertility and weather. Wild ginseng grows in our forests and steep narrow valleys. A root needs to be seven to ten years old to be the size worth digging commercially. People who have dug "seng" all their lives tell of finding large roots that could be sixty years old. Our ginseng is highly popular in China, where it is used for everything from indigestion to sexual problems. The chemical in the root of our ginseng is more than twice as concentrated as any other in the world. The dried root brings a hefty price. Two years ago dealers were paying $800 a pound.

Tobacco is raised in the central part of the Driftless Area. This is Type 55 tobacco, used for high quality cigars and chewing tobacco. In southern Wisconsin, Type 54 tobacco is raised. Identical seed is used but the final product is different. Type 55 will absorb twice as much sweetener when chewing tobacco is manufactured. The only reason would be our unique combination of soil and weather.

Another crop that we are not proud of is marijuana. This is highly illegal but is grown anyway in out-of-the-way places hidden from the public. There are people serving long prison sentences for raising "weed," and they got caught because they were doing it commercially and spending the profits big time.

If on the outside you are an ordinary farmer but all of a sudden are driving high priced sports cars and vacationing in Las Vegas or Hawaii, something looks very suspicious. We heard of one couple who raised half an acre of "weed" and did not get caught. They took home one million dollars! They then quit this crop and properly invested this gold mine. The first thing they purchased was a new house in the city. Paid cash. They then enrolled in college and got business degrees. Paid cash. They purchased two new cars to match their new house. Paid cash. Now they had no debts. Money in the bank. College degrees. And a past that no longer existed. They worked their way into the corporate world.

All well and fine, but to do this you cannot have a conscience. After all, they furnished an illegal drug that may have ruined the lives of hundreds of young people. Incidentally they never used the drug themselves.

A new wave of people are now moving into our area. They have "discovered" the Driftless Area and want to be part of the whole beautiful scenic picture. Sometimes they need an attitude adjustment. Those of us who have been here all our lives trust everyone. No one locks their door or takes the key out of their car. Most of the city people who come in and buy a piece of paradise in the woods are suspicious of their neighbors and the first thing they do is put up glaring signs all over their new property: No Trespassing—No Hunting—Keep Out—Trespassers Will Be Prosecuted.

The new house may be built on a steep hillside with a narrow winding road up to a basement garage. This may look clever and unique, but practically speaking, the owners create a big built-in problem for themselves, if they expect snow removal and fire protection. In the past, every time snow plows came out, driveways were all plowed when it snowed. But when the township was confronted with all those narrow steep driveways, they said, "There's no turnaround for the plow so we cannot plow your driveway at all."

The next problem was fire protection. With these narrow hillside drives you could not get fire trucks in. The fire chief went around to the new homes and explained that there was a county ordinance about driveways being two rods wide (33 feet). Sometimes he was met with hostility. The next time he came he brought an insurance man with him who explained: "If a fire truck cannot get in, we will cancel your insurance. Furthermore if your house burns and catches the woods on fire and spreads to your neighbor and burns his barn and house, you are liable and you could be sued for everything you could earn for the rest of your life."

Everyone saw the light and said, "I didn't realize" and "I want to be a good neighbor and comply." Now when someone builds a house in the woods, access is part of the package deal when they go to the bank.

Most of our new neighbors are well-educated, talented people. Some are authors and environmentalists and good neighbors. Some are couples who waited too long to retire and are in the grips of old age and failing health. In just a few years one or the other will pass away and their mate will move away and we'll never hear from them again. We feel that people should retire while they still have a good share of their lives left to live. The Driftless Area is a retiree's dream.

Country Gardens, Country Food

When my parents got married my mother, Ruby, was not prepared for what she was getting into. The Jasperson family lived frugally. Her mother, Sophia, traded cream and eggs for groceries purchased in town and spent a total of between forty and fifty dollars a year. They operated on the philosophy of "waste and ye shall want." The children's plates were dished up with the proper amount of food and they were expected to eat every last drop. There were no second helpings and no leftovers. You did not question it either because what their father, Andrew, said was law. If you complained you were sent to bed without supper. If you came to supper one-half minute late you were sent to bed, without supper. Mealtime was not a happy time in the Jasperson household.

In the Fortney home you never knew for sure how many would be there for dinner or supper. At times upwards of twenty people were staying in the house, plus unannounced company from "up north" or from Richland County to stay for a week or two. Grandma said, "Don't worry, we can feed them." Where could they all sit? Grandma said, "We can set the table twice, even three times if necessary." Ruby could not comprehend this. Fortneys were serving more food in one meal than the Jaspersons consumed in a whole month!

Grandma kept the wood stove roaring from morning till night. A normal breakfast for all these people would use three dozen eggs or more, three pounds of bacon, three loaves of bread, a pint jar of jam or jelly, two pounds of butter or more, two gallons of milk and thirty cups of coffee. The coffee was brewed in a sixty-cup boiler that took one pound of coffee to a fill. There would also be side pork and sometimes mashed potatoes and gravy. Of course molasses and honey were always available. Sometimes Grandma made buckwheat pancakes. Grandma and Grandpa raised one small field of buckwheat and saved it in a special bin in the granary. They took the buckwheat to the water-powered mill at Towerville to be ground into flour.

The eight o'clock breakfast would keep the hungry men going until morning coffee at 10:30. By this time Grandma would have baked a couple of coffee cakes while starting a batch of bread. The Fortney farm used at least twenty loaves of bread a week. Bread was baked every day except Saturday and Sunday. I can remember seeing ten one-hundred-pound sacks of flour stored in the sewing room closet.

Ruby by now was almost terrorized by what she had walked into in marriage. Not to be beaten by a challenge she said, "If they can do it, so can I!" But she never outgrew the Jasperson philosophy of "waste and ye shall want."

Grandma Karn said, "There is no such thing as waste. We fill a sixteen-quart garbage pail and feed it to the hogs, which we butcher and eat, so we make plenty and feed everybody and they're all happy."

A little note about the garbage pail, though: When we had hired girls on the farm, you could never trust them to sort what went into the pail. Before you fed the hogs you had to check the feed trough for forks, spoons and paring knives. The hired girls threw all kinds of odd things in the garbage.

Garden time comes in the spring, the season of renewal and hope. Seeds were saved from the previous year. Some seeds, of course, had to be purchased in town, but some, like potatoes, had to be from your own stock. You were considered a failure, your garden the result of poor planning, if you ran out of potatoes and had no seed stock. Getting potato-growing just right was almost a religious ceremony. The unwritten law of the land was that potatoes must be planted by Good Friday in the light of the moon and the ground could only be fertilized with horse manure.

Dad said, "That is all superstition and old wives' tales! It doesn't matter if you plant in the light of the moon or the dark of the moon, you just plant them in the ground. Wait until the ground is warm and they will come right up before the weeds get started." You know, he was right.

Fred in the strawberries. Yum! Yum! Yum!

Mother got educated about the size of a farm garden needed to feed the hordes of people that passed through our yard and house. Grandma planned in advance for a garden of almost one-half acre. In addition, a quarter-acre potato patch was in another location, and there was a strawberry patch and a raspberry patch. In the orchard north of the house were sixteen apple trees, four red plum trees and two big purple plum trees. This was almost too much to handle already, but there were six or eight more plum trees in the southeast corner of the lawn under the big oak tree. Out in the woods you could find endless wild blackberry bushes that needed picking, and down in the valley Grandma had a rhubarb patch, two rows each about thirty feet in length. Grandma knew of spots where wild red raspberries grew and other hiding places where gooseberries were thick. Gooseberries were picked green for sauce. They were so tart that your teeth felt like they had hair on them. After the gooseberries ripened, about the time blackberries were ripe, when they were a deep purple color, they made beautiful jelly.

There are two kinds of wild gooseberries, smooth-skinned berries and the kind with thorns on the berries. Grandma said, "The thorny one is best. They are sweeter and more tangy." Nobody agreed with her, but she picked them anyway. To get the spines off you would put them in an old stocking and rub and roll them, almost forever, it seemed like. We kids still wouldn't eat them, because one or two thorny spines might get missed and you would get that horrible spine ball in your mouth and maybe stuck in your throat. Mother agreed with us and never picked those horrible things.

There were several other foods that she didn't like—kidney pie, liver pudding and blood sausage. She told Grandma, "Either these things disappear or I am gone!" Grandma was surprised by Ruby's speaking up like that, but was pleased that Fred's new wife had a lot of spunk. Those nasty foods disappeared.

Raising the garden was a running battle to fight weeds and bugs. Ruby didn't let the hired girls hoe the garden because they couldn't tell the difference between vegetables and weeds. It seemed like the womenfolk were canning food all summer, vegetables and fruit juices and sauce. In the summertime there were more mouths to feed. This took a big bite out of the garden. When fall came, this was the time to butcher. They sometimes butchered six hogs. The hams, shoulders and bacon were smoked in the smoke house located on the edge of the orchard. Dad would cut down a hickory tree for wood to burn. The finished smoked meat would be hung from the rafters in the attic. The rest of the pork was canned in one-quart and two-quart glass jars.

The next butchering project would be a beef or two. This wasn't done until cold weather so the meat could be frozen hard. Another specialty was veal. Certain bull calves were allowed to nurse until they weighed at least two hundred pounds. Veal was a special treat, served for special company like the preacher and his family or relatives from far away.

We had a cold box on the north side of the house made of oak lumber and insulated with about eight inches of old newspaper and that worked quite well to store meat, as long as the weather stayed cold. Of course a lot of beef was canned and stored in the basement, a most delicious and tender treat. If any meat was left in the cold box come spring, it had to be cooked and canned before it started to spoil.

When winter set in, in December, we had a good stock of food on hand. In the attic would be up to twelve hams and twelve smoked picnics and ten slabs of bacon. In the basement you could find a huge bin with more than three thousand pounds of potatoes in it. On the shelves stood glass jars full of canned beef and pork, vegetables and fruit, and two-quart jars of applesauce, blackberry sauce, peach sauce and blueberry sauce, more than five hundred quarts in all, plus one hundred jars of jams and jelly, a forty gallon stone jar of sauerkraut and another stone jar filled with pickled pigsfeet, pork shank ends, and side pork packed in lard. There was a large bin filled with squash and pumpkins and stems of spices hanging from the ceiling.

Peaches in season were available in town and we always bought five or six crates. We didn't always have blueberries, but sometimes people would get together and go up north and pick almost endless amounts of berries. They grew wild in the swamps and there were blueberries as far as you could see. Some people brought along a stove and glass jars and canned them right there. They stayed in tents at night and picked again the next day.

The other end of the basement was piled clear to the ceiling with firewood and a short distance from the furnace was a pile of kindling for starting fires. The kindling came from old lumber saved just for this purpose.

We will now go back to the attic. The menfolks had selected choice ears of corn to save for seed and these were hung on nails on boards that lined the attic on three sides. They also saved their own tobacco seed. Paper bags were tied over the seed heads on choice plants. When they were partially dry the seed head was cut off and brought up to the attic to dry further.

The house was now ready for winter. We had most of a year's supply of food stored up, wood stored to keep us warm all winter, and some of the most important seeds stored inside the house. What else did a family need, besides coffee, salt, pepper and sugar? We had almost everything we needed right there at home. This would all change in ways that we could never have comprehended at that time.

Ruby got into the spirit of this way of living and did a great job of it. There were times, though, I am sure, that she would have liked to kill some of the stupid hired girls who came and went.

Premost

Premost is a soft cheese spread made by Scandinavians from whey. In Norwegian, "prem" (from "bream") means "spread" and "ost" means "cheese." (Sometimes you see "premost" spelled "bremost.")

My early remembrances of premost involve an old lady named Carrie Dregne who lived in Hinkst Hollow right below the Hinkst School. Carrie was a widow who lived with her two sons, Harold and Alfred. We were afraid of Alfred because he had seizures and could become quite violent. Carrie could usually quiet him down, though, and she was the only one that could control him.

Carrie made the most delicious premost, according to the method she had learned from her mother in Norway. A large kettle was required. Copper was best, but a large cast iron kettle would do. The whole process was carried out outside the house, over an open fire, and would take almost a whole day. Harold would go to the Liberty Pole cheese factory and get three or four ten-gallon milk cans full of sweet whey, a byproduct of making cheese. The cheese factory did not charge for the whey since it was considered a waste product.

The copper kettle was suspended over the fire by a tripod and chain. The fire underneath was very carefully controlled since the temperature had to be almost boiling, but not quite. Carrie did not use a thermometer to check the temperature of the sweet whey in the kettle, but I am sure if she had it would have been between 190 and 205 degrees. If your kettle started to boil, the product would scorch and taste terrible.

Carrie very carefully sorted her firewood and knew just what to put on the fire to get it right. If you needed a hot fire you would use old oak fence posts, but the fire could get too hot unless you had other wood to add. Harold would have other wood piled up for his mother. "Pole wood" often was used. This included ironwood, maple, hickory and sometimes box elder. If this wood was "green," just recently cut, it would burn slowly, and last. Pole wood, by the way, is from trees that are small enough so you can cut them down with an axe and most of the time you do not have to split the wood to get it into the kitchen stove.

By now Carrie has been stirring the kettle for several hours with a wooden paddle used just for this purpose and the liquid is reducing in volume. This continues until late in the afternoon and by then the aroma is indescribably pleasant. People driving by notice that Carrie is making premost, the word gets around the neighborhood and everybody makes plans to go down to Hinkst Hollow to get some of that good stuff.

It is getting toward evening and Carrie's premost is just about done. She covers the kettle and puts out the fire. By morning the premost will be cooled down and will thicken up so she can form it into small loaves about one pound in weight. Each loaf is carefully wrapped in wax paper and made ready for sale. Carrie's premost, sliced and put on fresh homemade bread, was most delicious. Premost has a sweet tangy taste and cannot be compared to any other cheese. It probably is unique unto itself. A stranger not Norwegian oftentimes is terribly shocked the first (and last) time he tastes it. It looks almost like peanut butter, but there is a world of difference in the taste.

The old method of making premost is a thing of the past. The old people that were specialists in this art have all passed away. Some years back there was a small attempt at factory-made premost, but it was a pitiful attempt to duplicate the masters. Nobody could stand to eat that garbage.

If old fashioned premost were available now, a true Norwegian who grew up on it would gladly drive two hundred miles out of his way to get a taste of it.

The Country Store

The country store is a hallmark institution of rural Wisconsin and rich in history. In our immediate area there seemed to have been one every few miles. Usually country stores were attracted to country cheese factories and the two became the glue that started a small village. A school came next, then homes and finally a church. Now you had the foundation of a small town. Invariably other businesses started, including blacksmith shops, small time implement dealers, automobile dealers, and then hotels, usually quite small, but still known for catering to travelers with a hot meal and a clean bed. Next came stores, with clothing and furniture and household notions. Some of these ventures lasted only a short time, if there was no call for their services. We will concentrate in this chapter on country stores. These stores were similar, but each was also unique unto itself. I will tell the story of the Liberty Pole store and then a bit about others in our vicinity and you will see similarities and also distinct differences.

Liberty Pole Store

Liberty Pole is a village in the Township of Franklin, Vernon County, Wisconsin, and is located on State Highways 27-82. The Driftless Area, as explained in a previous chapter, was mostly timber and wilderness except for a narrow strip about fifteen miles east of the Mississippi River. This was open prairie. The Indians routinely burned off the tall grass to keep the prairie open and to afford green pastures for the herds of bison and elk that they depended on for food and sustenance. Liberty Pole is located at the southern edge of this prairie. Even today you can see where the prairie ends and the timber starts. Nature always seems to erase men's transgressions and return the earth to normal.

Liberty Pole has the distinction of having been the site of the first permanent house built in Vernon County. It had the first post office, located inside the first store, which opened for business in 1845. This store has been open almost continuously ever since. It has changed much over the years to accommodate people's needs. When first opened, the store offered pioneering necessities such as gunpowder and bullets, rifles and shotguns, animal traps, knives, and other items along those lines. Later, when more settlers appeared, there were different needs, such as for basic kitchen items—kettles and pans, salt, pepper and sugar, coffee and, later, bacon and sandwich meat. The meat slicer was hand-powered, probably dating back to before electric lights. As you turned the handle, a round blade would turn and shave off a slice of meat, which would drop onto a properly placed wax paper to be sterile and clean. Between uses the machine would be out in the open air and the blade was never cleaned. Nobody complained and nobody ever got sick.

The slicer was sold at the Cade estate sale, a real prize for the new owner.

The Liberty Pole store sold shoes of all kinds, including special sizes for specific people. They even carried size 14 five-buckle overshoes. This size was not available in town, but the Liberty Pole store stocked them for certain farmers. People came many miles to get new boots because they knew Bill Schmidt always had them on hand. The store also had high-heel button-up shoes and patent leather shoes for little girls. At the Cade estate sale the Amish buyers bought up most of these patent leather shoes for their daughters, some buyers purchasing up to twenty pairs each. The Amish do not wear tennis shoes or any shoe with rubber soles. They consider them to be products of the Devil because they are close to the same material as rubber tires, strictly forbidden by their church.

Some stores sold beer as well as supplies, groceries and gas. It was against the law to sell beer in the town of Franklin. Our township was voted "dry" more than one hundred years ago, in the 1880s. Newcomers have tried to change the law many times, but they always fail when it comes up for a vote.

Folsom Store

Another store close to home was the Folsom store. This too was a general store with all the little things that farmers needed, but it also was a post office and it was located right next to the Folsom cheese factory. A perfect combination: Deliver your milk to the cheese factory, pick up your mail, buy a few groceries and charge them. When milk check day came around, the storekeeper would cash your check for you, taking out what you owed him for groceries.

Mason City Store

The Mason City store was somewhat different. It was located right on Highway 14, before the highway was rebuilt and relocated. (Mason City was not a city at all, but a store.) They had "Cozy Cabins," twelve tourist cabins for travelers that were small, with just enough room for a bed and a small table and chair. Each cabin had one lightbulb and one cabin also had a water faucet and a simple shower. The store was always open until 9:00 PM and you could buy certain groceries to get you by until morning.

Albert Ekum built the store, with living quarters attached, in 1920. When he first built it, on the north side was a hitching post where you could tie up your horses when you stopped. Later on, when cars became more popular, Albert tore the hitching posts out and built facilities to change oil and grease your car. It was about this time that the Cozy Cabins were built.

Mason City also was a pickup point for cream. At that time some people separated their milk and just sold cream. A truck would come out every day and pick up the cream and take it to the

Carnation plant in town. We used to go over to the Mason City store at night after chores. You didn't need to clean up, just go right from the barn, jump in the pickup and go. Soda pop was five cents a bottle and ice cream was twenty cents a pint. Everybody came and sat around and joked and told tall tales. We didn't have TV or computers to keep us occupied. At night we went to either Mason City or Liberty Pole for a good time.

During the 1940s Cozy Cabins were occupied every night. They filled a need, as there were practically no other places to stay while traveling in Vernon County.

West Prairie Store

West Prairie had an interesting store, located at the intersection of Wisconsin Highway 82 and County Highway N. Robert Felde wrote a book about this store titled Life at the Crossroads. The author's grandfather, Allen Halverson, opened the West Prairie store in 1894 and operated it all his life until he passed away in 1947, and then his son Alfred and daughter Ruth took over. That same year, Halverson's youngest daughter, Helen, and her husband, Lee Felde, moved into the living quarters connected to the store, and the two couples operated the store. In 1950, Robert Felde was born to Helen and Lee Felde, so he "lived" the story of the store. It was almost like the center of the world for many kids at West Prairie. The story really tugs at your heartstrings as you read the book. It was the unofficial morning coffee club for many of the neighbors. They sat around and told tall tales and gossiped about those who were not present. Aunt Ruth always had lunch for the mailman and the bread truck man when they arrived. Robert Felde said, "We probably would have made more money if we had charged for coffee and given away the groceries."

One problem West Prairie had, as did most country storekeepers, was extending credit and trying to collect on the bill. Alfred Halverson had one customer who had just moved into the area. They were a large family and dirt poor. Evidently they moved from place to place, whenever their credit ran out. Alfred, who was quite compassionate, told the man, "Sure, I will give you some credit. Just pay me when you get paid." These people had not eaten a full meal for some time and they picked out a huge amount of groceries. In about a week they came back for more, with never a hint about paying on the bill. Just before Christmas they came in again and the man told Alfred, "I really appreciate the credit you have extended to me and my family, so I am giving you a gift for Christmas." Alfred thanked him and put the wrapped gift under his Christmas tree. When he opened it on Christmas Eve, he found a bottle of shaving lotion, the very one the customer had "bought" at the store and charged. This family moved away soon after that, without ever having paid a dime on all that they had charged at the store. Robert Felde tells the story so vividly that you feel you are right in the story with him.

Two Stores at Avalanche

Down at Avalanche, Wisconsin, there were two stores at one time. One store had a tavern connected to it and had people coming and going all the time. Outdoor movies used to be quite popular. The storekeeper was in charge of the movie, a new one every night. There also was a "serial" show, a part of the story every night. You had to come very night for a week to see it all.

The other store was owned by Norman Skundberg. He had the same problem as others—people would charge and then "forget" to pay. One night, during a fierce thunderstorm, Norman's store was struck by lightning and burned to the ground. All the customers that owed money to the store completely forgot about Norman and he was left holding the bag. Years ago there were no food stamps or welfare so poor people just suffered.

Rising Sun Store

Rising Sun, a settlement located just over the line in Crawford County, has a lot of history. At one time they had a hotel, cheese factory, implement dealer, barbershop, Catholic church, dance hall, general store and saloon. One year the township of Utica in Crawford County voted to close all taverns and bars and be considered dry. This didn't bother the Rising Sun tavern. The next day the tavernkeeper and all his regular customers organized the Rising Sun Sportsman's Club. Membership cost $1.00 for life and members could bring guests. The club was open until 1:00 AM every day except Sunday. At the next election the people voted taverns in again. Maybe the police department would now have more control over public drunkenness.

The Rising Sun store was right across the highway from the tavern. They had everything a person could need. When the store first opened, horse and buggy was the form of transportation used. A boardwalk had been built in front of the store so you could just step out of your buggy onto the boardwalk. The ladies really liked this. But eventually the highway had to be improved, and this created a low spot in front of the store. When the highway crew finished digging, the door to the store was almost seven feet up in the air. The customers' first thought was, this is horrible, how can we ever get into the store? Building a stairway was not an option, as everybody was used to the nice boardwalk.

Someone came up with an idea to dig out under the store and make a downstairs floor, so that is what they did. Everybody in town came and dug and hauled dirt. They laid up a concrete walk and a new door and front windows and then moved the store downstairs. The former store space, now upstairs, was turned into a dance hall where the young people had a good time every Saturday night.

The Rising Sun store served a triple purpose, as general store, post office and telephone switchboard. Today the border between two big telephone companies is the highway that goes past the store. If you want to call your neighbor across the street you have to call long distance.

Rising Sun, like so many small villages around the country, is now just a bump in the road and you would hardly know that at one time it was a thriving community. The cheese factory burned down. The implement business folded. The dance hall was condemned because there was only one way to get out in case of fire. The post office closed years ago. The barbershop closed and a few years ago the store closed, never to open again. Just recently the tavern also closed, so all that is left are six or seven houses.

There were stores up and down these deep valleys that could not make a living so they just folded up. The country store life is a memory now, but it is a bittersweet memory.

Weird Words: Horse Terminology

When a young country boy grew up on a farm, he heard and understood the words spoken by grownups around him every day. City boys never heard these words and even their parents didn't know what the country boy was talking about. We will explore some of the horse terminology in use when I was growing up.

1. Bog spavin
2. Founder
3. Thrush
4. Wind broke
5. Night blind
6. Skitterish
7. Cribbing
8. Cupier
9. Collar
10. Check rein
11. Tugs
12. Hames
13. Blinder
14. Belly band
15. Lines
16. Butter of antimony
17. Proud flesh
18. Frog
19. Hoof rot
20. Colic
21. Drop two, drop four

If you grew up in town, this might look like a foreign language. If you will read on, I will explain what these words mean.

1. <u>Bog spavin</u>. Horses are prone to get sore feet when they work hard. Bog spavin is a deep bruise which, if infected, is very hard to heal. ("Spavin" is from Old French <u>espavain</u>, "swelling.")

2. <u>Founder</u>. Horses tend to overeat on good tasting food that they should not have, like cow feed or chicken feed. They are a single stomached animal and cannot vomit, so they get very sick, since this food just lies in the stomach and rots. A good horse doctor knows how to treat them. Horses can also founder on cold water, if you let them drink their fill before they cool down. If a horse drinks fifteen gallons of cold water, it will stop sweating and its body temperature will drop to dangerous levels. It could even die.

3. <u>Thrush</u>. This is another problem of neglected feet. It is a bacterial infection of the frog (the shock absorber of the horse's foot), with a smelly black discharge.

4. <u>Wind broke</u>. A condition like asthma, with respiratory tract and lungs irritated by dusty or moldy hay.

5. <u>Night blind</u>. Old horses get cataracts in their eyes plus vitamin deficiency and are blind at night. If frightened they run into fences, fall into ditches and get badly hurt. It is best to tie them up at night.

6. <u>Skitterish</u>. Some horses are nervous and are spooked by strange noises or by strange places. They can be dangerous to be around.

7. <u>Cribbing</u>. When horses are tied up in the barn they get bored and will chew on their manger. Cribbing, or crib-biting, is a bad habit and hard to break. They may chew up everything they can reach.

8. <u>Cupier</u>. A piece of harness that goes under the horse's tail.

9. <u>Collar</u>. The piece of harness that goes on first, arching the horse's head. It is padded, goes against the horse's shoulders and is buckled at the top.

10. <u>Check rein</u>. A leather strap that goes from the bridle to harness main strap to keep the horse's head up when being driven.

11. <u>Tug</u>. A heavy thick leather strip that goes from the harness to the wagon hitch to pull the load. Also called "trace."

12. <u>Hames</u>. A piece of the harness that straps to the collar and is the pull point for the tugs.

13. <u>Blinders</u>. Part of the workhorse's bridle. Leather flaps designed so the horse can see only to the front.

14. <u>Belly band</u>. A wide leather strap that goes around the horse's chest to hold the harness on securely.

15. <u>Lines</u>. Leather straps that extend from the horse's bridles to the driver on the wagon. If you have an eight-horse hitch, you may have as many as six lines to handle to control all eight horses.

16. <u>Butter of antimony</u>. A very caustic substance used to clean out horses' feet that are infected with hoof rot. When applied to the infected foot, the reaction causes smoke to rise. I don't think you can get it anymore; it is probably outlawed. (Butter of antimony, or antimony trichloride ($SbCl3$), is a soft solid which, when mixed with water, or otherwise moisturized, hydrolyzes and becomes HCl or hydrochloric acid. It was also used to dissolve and remove horn stubs from calves, so the farmer did not have to cut the horns off.)

17. <u>Proud flesh</u>. Horses have thin skin and a wire cut can be very serious. The skin will part and expose a wide area of flesh. This will not heal by itself and needs to be disinfected, stitched up and bandaged. The bandage has to be checked every day and watched for flies. If flies lay eggs in a sore, the maggots make the horse's skin problems even worse. On Kentucky horse farms nobody uses

barbed wire for horse fences because of the danger of wire cuts. They use only board fences.

18. <u>Frog</u>. This is the center of a horse's foot that is the connective tissue connecting the hard parts of the foot to the leg bone. This soft padding is the foot's shock absorber and needs to be cared for routinely.

19. <u>Hoof rot</u>. A condition of horse's feet caused mostly by neglect. Hoof rot, also called canker, occurs when a horse is kept in wet or dirty conditions. Like thrush, it results in a foul odor and discharge.

20. <u>Colic</u>. Stomach ache due to eating either too much or the wrong thing. Colic ranges from mild to severe and even fatal, if the bowel becomes twisted, bloated or impacted.

21. <u>Drop two, drop four</u>. When hitching up a team to a wagon and you ask the boss, "How do you hitch these horses?" and the owner says, "On the left horse drop two and on the right horse drop four," what does this mean? The end of the tug has a section of chain in it. The links are oblong and about two inches long. "Drop two" means to hook up to the third link and let two links hang down. "Drop four" means hook up to the first link and let four links hang down. This gives you an adjustment between horses if they don't pull equally.

A Year on the Farm

I remember our involvement with farming as we were growing up. Since we lived on a dairy and tobacco farm, everything we did had to follow a pattern with the weather for complete success. The old saying, "For everything there is a time and a season," still rings true about farming.

I will review a typical year on our farm in southwest Wisconsin, starting on March first. The sun is starting to warm up the earth and melt the snow and ice. Dad is itching to get started with something besides milking and feeding cows. We can always go to the woods and cut fence posts and also wood for next winter. Cutting and splitting oak fence posts is probably now a lost art. First off, the only native wood that makes a decent lasting post is white oak. You select a tree that is about sixteen inches in diameter at the bottom, quite straight and long up to the first branch. After you cut down the tree you study out what you have to work with. If the tree is thick at the bottom you may want to make "set posts" out of the lower end of the tree. A set post is one that you dig a hole for, and this post will be used for corner posts and brace posts. These will have to be cut six feet long. As the tree trunk gets smaller, the rest will be "drive posts," cut to a length of five-and-a-half feet, sharpened at one end, and driven into the ground to build or repair a fence in the spring when the ground is soft and damp. A thinking farmer always cuts posts a year in advance and piles them up to dry.

Now that you have decided on length of cut, the next process is to split the posts out of these lengths of log. You will need a pail of steel wedges and an eight-pound splitting maul. Old rusty wedges work best because when you drive them into the log they don't fly out again. Dad always said, "If you buy new wedges, don't put them away in the shop or the shed, but put them in an old pail on a stump in the woods so when it rains they will get rusty. After several years they will get pitted and they just get better with age."

Now, when you split a post log, you first study the grain on the end and look for a lateral fault, and that is where you drive in the first wedge. As you pound it in you will hear snapping and cracking as the log starts to crack open. The next wedge will go in the crack that you just made. As you hammer in the wedge you may want to start another wedge in the crack in the log. The snapping and cracking gets louder and louder and all of a sudden the log splits open into two halves. Each half can be split into three posts. As the tree gets smaller you may split each chunk into four parts and finally into two posts. If the tree had some real straight limbs, they too would make posts. Generally speaking, though, those limbs are real hard to split because they have been whipped around by the wind and the cross grain in the wood is just about impossible to split.

Now the rest of the tree can be cut up for firewood. This is real easy if you have a chain saw. The small branches go into a brush pile. Brush piles from several trees make excellent hiding places for rabbits.

Now look back at what you did with this tree that was not big enough for a commercial log. You could have a pile of twenty-two to thirty-five fence posts, a cord of fire wood, and a brush pile for rabbits.

Now it is coffee time. Ma sent along a thermos of hot coffee, a basketful of ham sandwiches and a can of fresh homemade peanut butter cookies. We can sit on a stump and enjoy the woods and listen to squirrels barking and watch woodpeckers and other birds that are looking for a place to build a nest. Dad and I visit about plans for the future and ideas about philosophy and religion. This is a special place for father and son to come and just be together. In today's world this kind of meeting just can't happen. Everything has to go fast and then there's barely enough time to get one thing done and go on to something else, sometimes seven days a week.

After we have our coffee we will pile up the posts properly against the stump. The posts must be piled up with the bark side down and piled so that air can circulate completely around them when it rains. The rain will get in under the bark and in one year when we come to get our posts the bark will be all loose and can be picked off by hand. The firewood can be racked up next to a tree. This too should be piled up bark side down. Next year when we haul this wood in, the bark will be all loose so we can leave it in the woods. Bark makes a lot of ashes and not much heat. If left in the woods it will rot down and make mulch for future young trees.

Dad always said, "We are stewards of the land and trees are a one-hundred-year crop. It is our responsibility to treat the woodland with respect and keep it healthy for all mankind in the future. Never cut all the trees and sell them. Someday you may have a fire and lose a building and right in your woods is a new barn that has been growing for the last hundred years. For fire wood, only cut down dead trees or trees that are defective. This will give the healthy trees room to grow. Also, trees that are completely mature should be harvested. They will make lumber, posts and firewood, and will open up the forest canopy for an explosion of new growth on the forest floor."

When we were kids, this kind of talk didn't make much sense, but now, after a lifetime on this farm, it is the gospel truth. If you respect Mother Nature, she will take care of you and your offspring in the future. Greed will only backfire and come back to haunt either you or your children.

Dad and I will now go home after a pleasant day in the woods. We will do chores early so the whole family can go to the 4-H meeting up at Belgium Ridge. I can tell the club about my day in the woods.

Dad always said, "Good fences make good neighbors." This wise old saying meant that if your cattle never got out and ruined your neighbor's crops, your neighbor's cattle couldn't get into your farm and do damage either. This made sense. We had a fence all the way around the whole farm plus many inside fences to divide the permanent pasture lots for the cows, hogs, horses and calves.

In the spring, before any field work starts, it is time to repair all the fences. If you are on the ball, you have a good supply of new oak fence posts on hand and you can load up a wagon with your posts and drive around the fences and inspect for weak or broken posts. You do this before the ground thaws out so you do not track up your fields. Just throw out a post wherever you need one and after the frost goes out and before you start spring plowing, you have a window of about two weeks to go around and drive in new posts and tighten up the barbed wire. You take out the broken posts and load them up in the wagon. What are you going to do with them, throw them in a ditch? Oh no, they are too valuable. They are perfect fuel for the steam engine.

A steam engine like the one that steamed our tobacco beds

Now have I lost you? What, you ask, is a steam engine used for? This is another process that most people today have no idea about. In our tobacco raising area, someone, I don't know who, discovered that if you injected live steam into the ground for the hotbeds for tobacco, the ground would be weed free!

This would be our next spring project, usually about the first week in April. It was always an exciting time for young boys. A big monster of a machine would roll slowly down the road driven by its owner. It usually had a steam whistle on it, maybe two whistles. When the driver pulled the wire for the whistle it sounded just like a train and little boys came running to see and hear this big, clanking, fire-breathing monster. Wood was burned to heat the water to produce steam for power. The fuel of choice was old white oak fence posts. There was a sort of sawmill right in the back of the machine where the operator would cut off one end of the old post to obtain a piece of wood about three-and-a-half feet long. It was the farmer's responsibility to furnish wood for fuel for this job. We had it on hand, the old fence posts that we had just gathered up from the fence we repaired.

The steam engine pulled in a steam pan, a rig sixteen feet long and almost six feet wide, with a homemade offset axle with a long handle which also acted as a hitch to pull the steam pan down the road. When you raised up the long handle (made from a piece of well pipe), the pan, which was made from metal and wood, would drop down on the newly plowed tobacco bed patch. The steamer had a long pipe plus a special steam hose to reach the pan.

The steamer man took great pride in making perfectly straight tobacco beds. He would drive in stakes at each end and sight along this line and if it met his satisfaction, dirt would be banked up around the pan and the steam turned on. In about twenty minutes the pan starts jumping, meaning that is all the steam it will take. Now the steamer man toots the engine whistle and everybody comes a-running to move the pan ahead. The live steam has gone almost two feet into the ground and has killed all the weeds and weed seeds and all the insects in the dirt plus warmed up the soil so the delicate tobacco seed will start right in growing.

When we were little, we always went and got several eggs from the chicken house and buried them in the dirt before the pan was moved ahead. After the pan moved past, we would dig up hard-boiled eggs. They tasted extra good and we ate them right there.

The other thing that the steamer needed was a lot of water. You would set up a stock tank near the machine and haul water in milk cans to fill it up. The steam engine had a steam-driven water pump to transfer the water to the boiler and to refill the storage tanks built into the machine.

We were reminded every year of how dangerous a steam engine is. If you let it get low on water so a flue was not covered, it could burn through in just minutes and live steam would be injected right into the fire at one hundred twenty pounds pressure. The result would be a horrible explosion and the whole thing would fly apart and kill anyone standing near. Mom always said, "Don't go near that dangerous machine. Stay far away."

Up on the Jasperson farm where she grew up, nobody steamed tobacco beds and their beds were all weeds and grass and the plants were terrible. Maybe they had never heard about steaming beds. After all, they did live ten miles away and their ancestors came from a different fjord in Norway, so maybe they weren't as smart as we were. Ha!

The next process was to set up the tobacco beds. We had sixteen-foot side board and stakes to hold them straight. Down the center of the bed was a wire stretched tight and stapled to center stakes. Next we smoothed out the sterilized soil and raked it all perfectly smooth. Tobacco seed is very very small. We never needed more than two ounces of seed for seven acres of crop. You would place the seed in a damp warm place, such as in back of the old cook stove, and wait for it to sprout. Then you would count out how many teaspoons of seed you had, divide by sixteen, and that was how much you needed for sixteen feet of bed. Dad always said, "Buy as much seed as you think you need and throw away half of it and you will have enough left to plant your tobacco beds."

How can you plant this tiny amount of seed in all of two hundred feet of beds? Simple! You mix it in the water in a sprinkling can, about a teaspoon in one fill, and use it up on sixteen feet of beds. Have faith, you cannot see any seed, but if the ground is evenly wet the seed is there. Now you need to put on the covers, thin muslin the length of the beds, fastened onto the boards with clothes-pins. Now you have to keep the tiny seeds moist until they grow to almost one inch tall. If you have a lot of windy hot weather you may have to water four times a day or more. If very tiny plants dry out they will all die. Incidentally, if every seed in one ounce of seed grew, it would plant more than twenty-five acres. You could sneeze and inhale five acres of tobacco and not even know it.

It will take six or seven weeks for the little plants to grow big enough to transplant. Now is the time to get to work and plant oats and corn and try to get some hay put up before tobacco planting time and also be able to cultivate the corn twice. This is the busiest time of the year and farm work comes first no matter what. If you can't stay on top of it you will get behind the eight ball and may stay behind for a whole year.

Years ago we didn't have modern chemicals and sprays, so it was a constant battle to stay ahead of weeds and bugs. Sometimes the weeds and bugs won and the farmer was the loser. If a big crop of weeds took over and went to seed, the ground was so contaminated that there was weed seed in the ground for the next fifty years and if you let weeds get the upper hand they would come back to haunt your children and their children, too. Just look at some of the organic fields of city boys turned farmer.

Now that all the crops are planted, what do you do to keep busy? It seemed like there was always a neighbor or a relative who got behind with his work, or got sick or hurt. It was common to get together for a "bee" and go over and plant his crops or harvest his hay for him. No one charged for this neighborly work. Who knows, maybe next year you would be in the same fix and they would all come over and bail you out. That is what neighbors are for.

Outside of chores with the cows, pigs and chickens, we also had to cultivate the corn and tobacco, hoe the tobacco and put up hay. If we got the first crop finished before tobacco planting, the second crop would be ready about mid-July. This was the best quality hay and the hottest time of year, so it dried fast, but you really worked up a sweat putting the hay in the barn. City boys didn't like to work on hot days. They just wanted to go to the swimming pool. We thought haying was the time to sweat and grow new muscles. After chores at night we might go down in the valley and jump in the creek. It was just us boys so we didn't need a swimsuit. We just stripped off and jumped in. The swimming pool uptown had too many rules, and we had none.

I heard about one time a bunch of boys went down to the creek for a swim, but there in the water was a bunch of girls skinny dipping. The girls didn't see them and the boys found their clothes and hid them, then went back to the creek and pretended to start to undress. The girls started to scream and went in deeper with only their heads sticking out of the water. The boys went up in the woods and hid and watched. Some of the girls were bawling as they came out of the water and couldn't find any clothes. They finally found them and dressed and went home. The boys laughed and laughed. Little did they know that the girls planned on getting even by doing the same to them. Finally they all went swimming together (skinny dipping). They had a lot of fun, and their parents never caught on.

In August, oats were ripe. We cut the oats with a grain binder. Only the Amish use grain binders today. Everybody else has used combines for the last fifty years. We used a tractor on the grain binder because it didn't get tired like horses and we didn't have to stop all the time and let it rest. The Amish farmers still have to stop because their horses get tired and hot.

After the grain is cut you have to shock it up to dry properly. A properly made shock will not fall down or blow over. We got stern orders on how to build a good shock. If people drove by and your grain shocks had fallen or blown over, they would tell everybody that the Fortney boys didn't know how to shock grain. That just could not happen. We felt we had a reputation to uphold. A shock consisted of nine bundles of grain—two center bundles, two bundles on each end of the shock, a brace bundle on each side and a cap bundle for the top. Never, never set a shock where running water might run through it and muddy up the straw. The cap bundle must be placed with the grain end facing the southwest (the direction most storms come from). Then the wind will be less likely to blow it off. The cap prevents rain from running into the shock and making the grain moldy.

Soon it was threshing time. My Uncle Malvin had a threshing machine and would thresh all the grain in the neighborhood. The farmers in his threshing run would get together and do "change work" among themselves (I help you and you help me). It was really fun work and everybody looked forward to threshing day. Malvin would pull in his big machine and either blow the straw into your barn or blow it into a stack outside.

Farm boys looked forward to the day when they would be old enough to go threshing. Part of the thrill of threshing was the big dinners that were served. When you came home at night the first thing Ma would ask was, "What did she serve for dinner?" Word got around fast. No woman would let someone else top her for the best or biggest dinner. By the end of the run the dinners were super banquets fit for a king!

It went the other way, too. Some renters had wives who didn't know how to cook and they probably had no money to buy many groceries. The crew would figure out a schedule so they could go to these farms soon after noon and work hard and be all done and gone before supper. Of course this poor farmer would be branded as the poor fool that married a stupid woman that didn't know how to cook.

I remember some hilarious things that happened during threshing days. One time they were threshing and blowing the straw into a barn. There was a guy up in the barn mowing away the straw. The thresher man decided to play a trick on him. He found an old jacket, a cap and a pair of gloves. He let out a blood curdling scream, then threw the jacket, cap and gloves into the machine. The guy in the mow thought somebody had fallen into the threshing machine and that parts of him were coming up the blower pipe! He came down from the mow white as a ghost and everybody laughed at him.

Another time they were threshing out by the field and the drinking water was in a milk pail by the machine. The water was all covered with chaff. A guy came along to get a drink. He pushed the chaff aside and took a dipper of water and proceeded to take a long drink. A couple of guys came running and yelling, "Don't drink that! The dog drank out of that pail." He ignored them, took another dip and drank that, too. They shouted, "Didn't you hear us?" To which he replied, "Didn't hurt the dog!"

Another story was not funny. An uncle told of what happened up in Monroe County. The crew was threshing at a farm and it was dinner time. On the way to the house, one guy was smoking a cigarette and flipped it over onto the road. A bird flew by and thought it was something to eat. He picked it up and flew away. The crew was just about done eating when somebody said, "Those are sure some strange clouds going over. The sky was clear when we came in." A couple of fellows went outside to see the strange clouds and came running back shouting, "The barn is on fire!" Evidently the bird that picked up the cigarette flew into the barn and dropped it in the haymow in the new fresh straw. They were lucky to get the threshing machine and wagons away from the barn before they all caught fire.

The next project on the farm was tobacco topping. When the tobacco plant starts to bloom you need to go through the field and break off the blossom and a little more from each plant. The idea is to leave twelve to fourteen leaves on each plant. Now all the grow power of the plant goes into the remaining leaves. In about three weeks is harvest time. In these three weeks the dry weight of the tobacco almost doubles.

Wild blackberries are also now ripe over in the woods. Dad loved to pick berries and sometimes he could pick two sixteen-quart pails full in a long afternoon. We had blackberries and cream and sugar every night and Mom canned a lot of berry sauce.

The next projects on the farm sometimes clashed. Some years, silo filling and tobacco harvest came at the same time. There just was not enough help around to do both at the same time. Tobacco had to be harvested when it was ripe and harvested in the same order that it was planted. If it was planted in ten days you had ten days to harvest. A thumb rule: Five good men should be able to harvest one acre in a ten-hour day. If your crew was made up of a bunch of children and some old grandpas, this would not be possible. Every year people would cuss the tobacco crop, since it was backbreaking work and too much risk. Sometimes a late hailstorm would come just as the crop was ready to harvest. Five minutes of hail and the crop was completely ruined and had no value.

Dad hired some of the same men every year and we always got the crop in in good shape.

Silo filling came next. We had a much bigger silo than everybody else in the neighborhood, so we had to do more change work than anyone else to get enough help to fill our own silo. By now the cow pasture was chewed down short and the cows were hungry. With the silo corn harvested we could pasture half of the farm and the cows thought they had gone to heaven.

In October we hired a neighbor to come and pick corn. Now the cows could have the other half of the farm. They always went up in milk in the fall.

Now farming was basically done for the year. We kids of course were back in school. The middle of September was Vernon County Fair time. We kids could hardly wait for the fair. Our fair was and still is the last (latest in the year) county fair in Wisconsin. It is a harvest fair and exhibitors bring in the very best of the very best of crops and livestock and the women bring in flowers and baking and sewing all to compete and try to get first prize. In the livestock area are the best cows and calves and pigs, chickens and sheep.

We boys were very interested in these things for a while, but by the time we were fourteen years old or so, something else began to interest us—girls! We put them in three categories. One group was the ones that felt they were so beautiful they didn't have to even talk to ordinary country boys. The next group was the girls who were bashful and pretty nice, and if we got up enough courage, if we dared to ask them, maybe they would ride on the Ferris wheel with us. The last group was the fat and ugly girls who were boy crazy and chased just about anything that walked. We stayed far away from them.

After a year at high school we got braver and braver. The next year at the fair was different and the young people were pairing off and going to dances and having a good time. Mothers always worry and mine warned me to "be a gentleman and do not take advantage of these sweet young girls." I knew what she was referring to, and my teaching from Sunday School always came to mind. Maybe Mother was young at one time, too, and remembered when she was growing up.

After the county fair was over, there was not a lot to do on the farm. At school we were making friends with a lot of new people, including girls. This was a new and exciting, but scary, experience. Some girls thought if you went out with them several times that you were going steady. Most of us boys didn't want that to happen because the girl got too possessive and you were put out of circulation. Maybe their intent was to get a mate, but we were not at all ready for that at our tender ages. It was a lot more fun to "play the field."

The next farm project was to "take down the tobacco." The tobacco was completely cured by now. After hanging in the tobacco shed for almost three months, it was brittle as glass and could not be handled until it softened up. When we got foggy weather, which was known as "case weather," the tobacco could be taken down and piled up in the shed. When the moisture was just right the leaves were as soft as silk and we piled them up in large round piles that held the moisture in.

We stripped the tobacco in the barn. Before the barn was remodeled the space in front of the horse stalls was perfect for stripping. We placed the tobacco leaves in a packing box lined with a special paper, and used three-cotton twines to tie the box up when full. Good tobacco would yield about thirty-six hands of tobacco, to make a fifty-pound bale. A "hand" of tobacco is the leaves from a lath of tobacco, about five plants. The laths are hung on a stripping rack and the leaves are picked off one at a time. This sounds like a boring job, but we listened to country western music on the radio, talked politics, and if there were no women around we told some pretty "ripe" jokes, too. The coffee pot was always on and we had a good time.

The aim every year was to get done stripping before Christmas. Then you would be free to go to all the parties with the girls and your other friends.

Soon after Christmas the tobacco buyers started coming to buy your crop. Read the chapter, "Tobacco, the Devil's Crop" to learn about marketing.

After Christmas was put away, the next thing to happen at Hinkst School was Valentine's Day. Teacher always made a valentine box to put valentines in. It seemed that some of the girls liked us boys only one day a year. You guessed it—only on Valentine's Day.

Spring is just around the corner with a promise of a new growing season. We are now one year older and one year wiser. The calendar has rolled around to the time of year when this story started and we are ready for whatever destiny has in store for us.

Changes: High School, Army, Marriage and Beyond

People were not as mobile in the 1930s and 1940s as they are nowadays. Church was every third Sunday, although Sunday School was every Sunday. You didn't go to town unless you had important business to tend to. Kids walked to school, only one and a quarter miles. If you went to high school, seven miles away, you stayed with relatives in town. We had electricity, a modern bathroom, and a good radio so we could listen to various programs and news. Mom was a trained nurse so she took care of all our aches and pains. Our little world was just about complete.

By the time Fred and I were old enough for high school, there were school buses that usually came right to our door. They were not as dependable as today and sometimes we waited and waited and the bus never came. The driver may have been running late and just skipped our road and gone straight to town. I drove to high school the last two years. I had my own car when I was sixteen years old.

In the local high school, the city kids looked down on us country kids. They thought we were a bunch of hicks. That didn't bother us, though. We knew better. When graduation came, most of the kids on the honor roll were country kids.

As years roll by, things change. As modern farming evolved we no longer needed a crew of hired men. Without all those people around we no longer needed hired girls. Dad purchased newer farm equipment and everything was a lot easier outside. It was time for a big change. Many of the hired men who worked for us had farm deferments and with the war over, they all hit the road and left Dad high and dry. But he just modernized and did without them.

Business was booming both in town as well as on the farm. You could take a load of hogs to town in your rickety old truck and then go to the truck dealer and trade for a new one and have change left out of your hog check. Today your hog check might buy a spare tire. The first thing Dad bought for the house was a deep freezer and a new refrigerator. Without so many people around we didn't need to store so much food and putting it in the freezer took just hours compared to many weeks of canning.

I remember 1946. The war was over and business was booming. We raised tobacco for a cash crop and Dad insisted that Mom deserved a fur coat. She kept saying she did not deserve such an expensive gift, but Dad insisted. We all went along to La Crosse to see her model fur coats and help decide on the right one. Finally she settled on a "Mouton Lamb" coat. It was a three-quarter length swing-style coat, light blue-gray in color, with cuffed raglan sleeves. It was beautiful and we were so proud. Many of our neighbors' wives got full length mink coats, but we thought Mom's coat was the prettiest.

Dad wanted to buy her an automatic washer and dryer set, but she would not hear of it, which was just as well, as the first ones were not dependable and very slow. With all the clothes around our house, you could have washed clothes all day and never got done. I am afraid Mom would have thrown it out and washed with the old Maytag wringer washer again.

We did, however, get a new radio. It was an AM-FM and short wave with a place to put a built-in TV if we got an area station sometime in the future. It also had an automatic record player. This was our entertainment center. It cost more than five hundred dollars, equivalent to five thousand dollars today. Next was a piano so Sue and Fred could practice and after that, a new carpet for the living room, a 100% wool rug. Actually we were just catching up on all the things we had done without during the years of the Second World War.

We kids were growing up too and getting itchy feet to see the rest of the world. I graduated from high school, was drafted into the United States Army and served a tour of duty in Korea. Fred went to college and Sue was in high school and David was in grade school. Mom and Dad really didn't have any help on the farm and they should have had a full-time hired man who could have at least taken over the barn chores. They did hire a young boy, but he did not know how to work and didn't understand that cows need to be taken care of seven days a week. His mother was always interfering and expected him to help her most of the time. She did always show up on Friday night to get his paycheck and kept insisting that the poor boy needed a raise.

I was on the other side of the world and could not do anything about the farm except worry. When I got out of the Army, I came right home and took over the farm. I had been gone eighteen months and was shocked to see how the folks had aged while I was gone. Both Dad and Mom were tired and exhausted and bent over and their hair had turned mostly gray.

This was a big change for me, too, after almost two years in the service with people around all the time and a lot of things to do. I was used to a lot of action and noise all the time. When I woke up after the first night at home, it was as silent as a tomb, with no people around. My first thought was that I couldn't hack this and for two cents, I would have walked out the door and never looked back and reenlisted in the Army. Even my old friends were gone. Some had moved away and others had got married. I was an odd duck in the wrong place. Suddenly a flood of guilt came across me. I had a responsibility to my family and all the time I was in Korea I had dreamed of the day when I got home and could farm the family farm.

We worked out a plan where I could rent the farm from the folks, and a contract where I would buy half the cattle and all the machinery. I became active in the 4-H Club as a leader and took a job as treasurer at our church. I was still regimented in military schedules as far as going to bed and getting up at the same time every day. The rest of the family didn't follow any schedule and I had to get mad a couple of times to get them to see what I expected.

Mom and Dad could now go on trips and relax a bit. For their twenty-fifth anniversary Dad bought a new car, a two-toned blue Buick Super 8 cylinder, and had it delivered on Sunday afternoon while we were celebrating their anniversary. Mom was completely surprised and overjoyed. Dad had been almost sick because he was afraid she would not approve. The new Buick was a beautiful car and very comfortable. They planned many trips around the state and to see relatives out west. This was the retirement they had always dreamed of, but Dad had a heart problem that was much worse than anyone knew. For years every time he sat down he would go to sleep, and always in church, too.

At our 4-H Club I met a cute girl that I just adored. We went together about two years and on August 16, 1958, we married. Her name was LaVonna Jane Fisher. Now my life had taken on a new meaning. We built a new house on the farm, all built from oak lumber cut in our woods. Dad was so proud of our new house. Dad and Mom were looking forward to the day when they would see grandchildren. Dad had not been feeling well and he went up to the hospital in the spring of 1960. While at the hospital he died of a massive heart attack. He was still young, sixty-four years old.

Our world was turned upside down. Dad never saw or held a grandchild. If we had had today's technology in 1960, Dad could have had a bypass operation and may have had twenty years more of life. We had reached another crossroad. Life would never again be like it was when we were children growing up.

Afterword

After Dad's funeral we pulled ourselves together and decided that Dad would want us to continue our lives in the way he had taught us, with self respect, compassion and concern for our fellow man, our families and our country, and the land that had given us our sustenance. He had told us, "We are only here for a short time. Leave the earth in better shape than you found it."

David, Sue, Fred and Tom in 2008

We were now ready to branch out and pursue our life's ambitions. I took over the farm and was the first in my family to get married. I married LaVonna Jane Fisher and we built a new house here on the farm a short distance from the big house. The house was built from lumber cut in our woods. My grandfather,

Ole T. Fortney, promised me when I was three years old that there would be trees for me to build a new house when I got married. Jane and I have three children—two boys, James and Ole, and a girl, Nicholine, named after my Danish grandmother. James has a job as maintenance supervisor for A Ready Mix Company. Ole is a technician for a dairy supply company. Nicki is a nurse practitioner for a large health care organization. They each have two children, so we have six grandchildren.

My brother Fred graduated from St. Olaf College at Northfield, Minnesota, with a teaching degree. After spending a tour of duty in the Navy and an interesting summer in Norway as an International Farm Youth Exchange student, he took a job teaching Latin. He married Donna Ellefson, an accomplished piano major and German teacher. They have two daughters, Maren and Elise, and four grandchildren. Maren graduated from Northwestern University with a degree in business and Elise graduated from Gustavus Adolphus College with an elementary teaching degree.

My brother David, who is a math whiz and a computer guru, teaches at a private school in Asheville, North Carolina. He married Julie Tracy, who also teaches. She has a doctor's degree in voice and teaches at a private college at Mars Hill, North Carolina. They have two boys, Michael and Matthew, who are not yet married.

My sister, Sue, went to school at Lawrence College at Appleton, Wisconsin. She has had a lifetime career in music with both piano and pipe organ. She is a church music director and organist and gives private lessons to students whose parents also took lessons from her when they were young. She married Peter Walby, who had a career in hospital management and now has a retirement career as a radio sports announcer for area schools. He is very good at it. They have a son and two daughters. Music comes as second nature to Sue and Peter's whole family. Their children are Chad, Catherine and Joan. Chad played the clarinet in high school band. Catherine is very talented in piano and now teaches piano at Lawrence College. Joan is a piano expert, too. Chad and Joan are married, but there are no grandchildren yet.

Dad would have been so proud of our family's musical talents, but he had only seen the start when he passed away. We have come a long way from when we played in the yard with kittens and puppies. The circle of life has revolved a full turn and now we stand in the circle where our grandparents were when we were growing up. One great advantage we have is that we can appreciate and enjoy our grandchildren. Ole T. died when I was three-and-a-half and Fred was just over two years old. Ole T. and Karn barely knew their grandchildren. Our oldest grandson, Carl, James's son, started high school in 2009, and we can observe him as he develops into a young man. We hope to be around to see him graduate from college and even see him get married someday. Maybe we will even get to know our great-grandchildren, something that as far as I know has never happened in our family.

Now I will close my rambling, since you have met all the people in this branch of the Fortney clan. My Army experience, and our grandchildren, are stories for another day.

Tom Fortney, April 2010